Shadow in the Forest

Leigh Swinbourne has been shortlisted for the Patrick White Playwrights' Award, the Varuna Award and the Tasmanian Literary Prizes. He has published two collections of stories – *The Shark* and *Away*. *Shadow in the Forest* is his first novel. Born and raised in Sydney, Leigh has lived with his family in Hobart since 2001.

For more on Leigh's writing, go to
www.leighswinbourne.com.au

Also by Leigh Swinbourne and published by Ginninderra Press
The Shark
Away

Leigh Swinbourne

Shadow in the Forest

Acknowledgements

An earlier version of this novel was the recipient of
a Varuna Longlines Fellowship.
The author wishes to acknowledge the generous assistance of
zoologist Dr Sarah Munks.

Shadow in the Forest
ISBN 978 1 76041 781 9
Copyright © Leigh Swinbourne 2019
Cover: Cathy McAuliffe Design

First published 2019 by
GINNINDERRA PRESS
PO Box 3461 Port Adelaide 5015
www.ginninderrapress.com.au

'You think that beasts are wholly without passions?' I asked her.
'Quite the reverse; we can communicate to them all the vices arising
in our own state of civilisation.'

Honoré de Balzac, 'A Passion in the Desert'

Prologue

Twilight, and the creatures of the Walls are abroad, stirred from warm diurnal slumbers by the imminent dark and hunger. A pademelon falters through a thick grove of pencil pines, ill, abandoned, seeking shelter amongst the twisted trees from a rising night wind. Its glossy pelt quivers with the sensitivity of fever, flinching at random dabs of snow. Occasionally it stoops to the neat carpet of grass between the pines, but the familiar food is sour, unpalatable.

Something.

The small being gathers into itself, leans back tensely on long legs and tail, raises its triangular head, sniffs the sharp air. Nothing but blood-beat dimming response. On again, paws and feet and tail, the cold heart of the forest always calling.

Something. Nothing.

Then a clearing in this densest part of the woods. The ancient pines meet high above in an ogive, creaking majestically, shutting out the tumult of the sky. The creature looks up and feels the ground swaying. In this space, prematurely, it is full night, the velvet darkness almost still, the blizzard howling without.

Paws, feet, tail, to where the pademelon sniffs stiff remains of kin. Something is wrong. Again the bunched concentration and failure to clarify. Then a sudden odour, an inconceivable flash of pain, and brief final knowledge as its throat is ripped out to the bone.

Passage

The plane looks small to Evelyn in the broad expanse of the aerodrome, but it is small, two engines with propellers, a veritable minnow compared to the sleek silver monsters roaring in the near distance. Yet like them this squat lump of metal will soon be airborne, be itself in fact, independent and free in the heavens, transporting a precious freight of life through an unstable, capricious medium.

Not a cloud. Where is this man she's meant to meet? Joseph Todd still hasn't appeared, twelve minutes past scheduled lift-off. Although she's never seen or spoken to him, Evelyn knows none of the other passengers standing here could possibly be a bushie, and nobody looks like they are looking for anyone else. They are composed, like bloody cattle, even though they are also wasting time like her. How do they manage it? Against their complacent stillness she cannot stop fidgeting.

The passenger nearest, a jowly tweed-clad sixty, seriously country, has a large wen on his ruddy left cheek. Now that she's noticed it, Evelyn can't stop glancing. She catches his eye and he nods companionably. She returns the acknowledgement before she can prevent herself. The last thing she wants this morning is to have to talk to one of these men, or anyone. At least her sunglasses give her some anonymity. She turns away towards the acres of glittering matt black, lets that empty distance soothe her.

It's good he's not going to turn up; her first stroke of luck for the day. There is always an unwelcome tension in meeting new people. She would have had to share a seat with him on the plane, and maybe even a hotel for a night in Devonport. Now, since he's not coming, she has needlessly endured this expectation of him.

Scanning the faces yet again, she cannot suppress a creeping dislike for these men. This is irrational: don't think about them, but of course being conscious of such a decision at once makes it impossible. They all start shuffling away from her; maybe she is radiating antipathy. A sleek antiseptic hostess and a sporty type with a clipped military moustache who must be the pilot have joined them. Finally they are boarding.

She is last in line. Forced proximity. Shouting from across the tarmac, a pang of displeasure as Evelyn knows without looking, it is the man she is meant to meet. Now she has readjusted to not meeting him. Not looking simply delays the inevitable, so she turns and takes him in.

Big and solid, not her physical type, yet he carries himself lightly, almost skipping in his enthusiasm with the uneven ballast of his luggage. No tie or coat, a ratty Wilderness Society T-shirt, army surplus pants, Blundstones naturally, and the inevitable beard, the badge of the bushie. His beard is short and curly, like his hair, and this with his round rosy face gives him a distinctly boyish look, at odds with his powerful man's body. Evelyn spontaneously likes him, and this is simply because he doesn't look like a man running to catch a plane, but someone with the greatest news in the world to tell. He comes up close, too close; he recognises her too. She smells his sweat, but it is fresh, almost sweet.

'You must be Evelyn Carter. Joseph Todd. Sorry I'm late.'

'Pleased to meet you.' She steps back and holds out her hand.

He shakes it uncertainly, his grip not as strong as hers. He is flushed but even so he reddens slightly, and Evelyn sees that despite his natural exuberance, he is shy.

'Looks like I just made it.' He laughs with relief and self-consciousness. 'Don't know my way around Sydney, I'm afraid.'

They both clamber in.

Evelyn sees that, inevitably, there are two remaining seats together. 'Do you mind if I take the window?' she asks. 'I like to watch the landscape.'

'Sure.'

They settle down. Strap in. The plane taxies down the runway, awkwardly, like a beast performing an unnatural task, then a pause, a rising intensifying whir, a swift burst of acceleration, the sudden banking that never fails to thrill Evelyn, and finally rising high above the orderly red-roofed suburbs, there is her little circumscribed world. At this height, the mess and destruction man has wreaked upon this once pristine landscape seems neat and rational, as though he really could impose sensible order there.

She had hoped for a view of the coast but it's the seaward side of the craft, and once they have steadied, all that's visible through the scratched double-glazing is the limitless blue of the Pacific. The immense wrinkled surface is lost in a distant chill haze, a melding of earth and sky, no horizon, no definition. Only if she strains around can she see the aluminium wing juddering noiselessly. This fragile little plane, not unlike fragile little earth in space.

'Anything out there?' Joseph is leaning over her shoulder.

Making herself smile, she faces him. 'A few cirrus clouds. A southerly's on the way. We'll probably fly into it.'

'Do you know the forecast for Tassie?'

'There's a large high over the island.'

'Let's hope it lasts.'

'I guess so. Although I'm sort of prejudiced against fine weather.'

At this odd remark, Joseph regards his new acquaintance seriously. Does she mean a joke, a witticism, or even a challenge? Who is this woman that Professor Atherton has praised so highly? In his mad scramble to make the plane, he'd almost forgotten about her. As usual, he'd totally underestimated the traffic and the distance. Sydney was huge compared to Hobart, endless miles of it.

Sitting at a constant succession of red lights on Southern Cross Drive, he'd completely given up. An idea never entertained by his taxi driver, garbed in djellaba and skullcap, sipping diet Coke, blasting out Triple J, and drumming his palms manically on the steering wheel ('Do you play in a band?' 'No sir.'), ducking and weaving, oblivious of horns and curses, and indeed, delivering Joseph to the airport just on time. Where the mysterious Evelyn Carter seemed to glare at him from behind forbidding sunglasses.

'But,' he says, trying to keep it going, 'wet in the wilderness is very inconvenient.'

'True.'

'Do you know the Walls at all?'

'No, I gather they're pretty exposed.'

'Believe me, you'll be grateful for fine weather.'

No doubt he's right, thinks Evelyn. He knows the area, she doesn't, although she has walked in his study area, Cradle Mountain, five years ago, a glorious student vacation. And like him, she is an experienced bushwalker. But yes, she wants no inconveniences. She is carrying a lot of gear, particularly her books and notes which might spoil in the damp, and she is not yet outstandingly fit.

'Will you be staying the night in Devonport?' she asks.

'No, I'll head straight out to the bush. Had enough of civilisation. Sydney's all a bit much for small-town boys like me.'

'I suppose you know Cradle Mountain pretty well.'

'Walked all over it since I was a kid. Still, the park covers a big area. I don't really know how useful my report is going to be. Your area's much more contained, more vulnerable too.'

'Because it's smaller?'

'Because it's alpine. Something else too: there's been camper reports of thylacine sightings from the Walls. They pop up every now and then, a bit like a rash. There might be a dog or something wandering around. When you go in, keep your eyes open.'

'The legendary long-vanished Tasmanian tiger. I'll tell you if I see one. Promise.'

'It's not a joke if there is a dog. Something will have to be done about it. Probably there's nothing at all, just the wilderness.'

'Just the wilderness. God, it's so good to get away from Sydney! You're lucky you don't live there. Such a hole.'

The bitterness of this surprises Joseph. He looks her over. Big-boned and lanky, strong but thin, restless, nails bitten to the quick. Doesn't seem to care much about appearance, and admittedly he finds this appealing. He likes the short, stiff brown hair uncombed, the outsize T-shirt and overalls. Student habits, no doubt. Pretty face, unusual somehow, looks very tired, end of degree probably (he was a wreck, he'll never forget it), still those grey eyes shine so fiercely and with obvious intelligence. Yes, thinks Joseph, you can clearly see the animal, and with the intelligence, rationality, such an intensely human compound. He has always been drawn to intensity, maybe because of his own personal hesitancies.

Evelyn shrinks, bridling at his gaze. She feels exposed, skinned. She turns back to the window, the bright smarting blue nothing. Three months in the wilderness, three whole months. Solitude, the glory of being alone, a chance finally to compose her mind. Now so particularly tempting since she has broken off yet another relationship, and this with the greatest hope invested. Surely, she remonstrates silently to the non-horizon, one is meant to become less vulnerable as life progresses, not more. Get tougher, conditioned.

She had been in the shower, glowing, when she made the decision. This was it, yes, cleanse herself of Graeme too. Why, if so much was right? Because of the little that was wrong, the little she knew she could never abide. Sooner or later, she would have to bite the bullet, so why not now before she leaves? How? Provoke an argument. What? A staple, a well-worn irreconcilable: her hatred of, his love of, the big city.

An only child, like her, but unlike her, growing up largely by himself on a farm near Bourke, Graeme loved the city, loved cohabiting with a shifting motley in some mouldering inner-city terrace, loved the cafés, traffic noise, the constant bustle; he even seemed to like the cockroaches. And he was a musician, a rank and file violinist with the Sydney Symphony, so the city was the heart of his professional life; he had no vocation outside it. With her leaving on this project, they were both on edge. Yes, this was the time.

'Just imagine being out there, Graeme! It seems so unnatural living in a world of concrete boxes!'

'Eve, why do you think cities exist? Because people obviously prefer to live like this.'

'That's stupid! They exist for economic reasons.'

'You're always carrying on about the natural world but immediately around us, Miss Zoologist, is the real miracle of evolution. Just imagine: single-cell organisms somehow eventually evolving into teeming cities, vast complicated structures where millions live and work together in peace, where at will we can get fresh food and hot water, where all our wastes are disposed of cleanly and efficiently, cities that have art galleries and concert halls. A single-cell organism all the way to *The Magic Flute* and *St Matthew's Passion*. We've even finally managed to dispense with God.'

'Bach and Mozart didn't dispense with God. All that's happened is we've made ourselves God.'

'Eve, there's nothing in the wilderness. We'll see how you feel about it after a few months.'

'Graeme, I don't want to see you when I get back.'

A quantum leap. By the look on his face, he'd obviously had no idea. She watched him slump slowly down on the bed, his head hanging; he knew she meant it. She felt so powerful standing there over him, wrapped only in a couple of towels, kicking him out. Bizarrely, she also felt slightly aroused, but also, inevitably, as she delivered her *coup de grâce*, she knew she was also cutting herself somewhere deep inside.

She shuts her eyes from the glare and descends within, senses the pain, stagnant waters below the foundations. Yes, she must come to terms with this, but it is too early; she is still in semi-shock mode, needing to escape. She is hoping that with this trip, among other things, space will assume the duty of time and help her forget. A fresh set of experiences sealing off one part of her life, so she can move on unencumbered to the next.

'Excuse me, madam.'

Joseph passes on a tray of sandwiches.

'Hungry?'

'Not especially.' She leans across to speak to the stewardess. 'Could you bring me a cup of coffee?'

'Certainly, madam. Milk and sugar?'

'Just black, thanks.'

'I'll have the same,' says Joseph. 'Evelyn, the Prof gave me the key to the cabinet in Dixon-Kingdom hut to hand over before I left Hobart.' He fishes around in his pants pocket. 'Here it is. Also, there's a drop waiting at the hut. Baits and traps largely. The Prof told me you're a zoologist. That right?'

'Yes.'

'Actually, I've read a couple of your mother's books.'

'What!'

'He also told me your mother's Janet Carter. While I was at uni, a girlfriend of mine took Women's Studies and she kept on about one of your mum's books, so I borrowed it. Found it interesting, so then I read *Towards a Peaceful World*. And that really helped inform my environmental thinking on a more global scale, helped me think beyond Tasmania.'

'Could we change the subject?'

'Sure.'

Although, she must remind herself, it is natural for people to ask about her mother. Still, pretty amazing to come across a guy who has read books like that. Not that she's ever managed to get through one. Formidable and airless.

'What were you doing in Sydney?' she asks.

'I flew up on behalf of the Wilderness Society. There are important conservation issues coming up in Tassie and a number of projects we're trying to get underway. We're keen to maintain the momentum after last year's Franklin victory.'

'Were you involved with that?'

'Very much. So I've been meeting with other conservation groups, explaining the issues, trying to coordinate resources. You should think about joining up with us when you get down to Hobart.'

'I don't know. Any commitment is such a big thing for me. I really do admire the work you do. It's so idealistic.'

'It has a serious practical relevance too.'

'Of course.'

Yes, of course, thinks Joseph. Serious practical relevance: how pompous that sounds, he's been listening to too much pollie-speak. Also, he shouldn't have gone on about the mother; obviously that didn't go down well.

'Your coffees, sir, madam.'

'Thanks.' Joseph attempts a smile as he passes hers over. 'I guess I mean,' he continues, 'that conservation is a hands-on business.'

'Sure.'

'Do you have a specific study subject?'

'What? For this project?'

'I assume the Prof has headhunted you for some reason.'

Headhunted? 'I've done work on lumpy jaw in macropods,' she replies. 'Apparently there's a problem with it up at the Walls.'

'How campers might be causing it?'

'Basically. My Honours thesis was on the Blue Mountains, and I looked at lumpy jaw there, among other things.'

'Remind me: this is an infection caused by the accumulation of soft food particles around teeth and gums.'

'Lack of fibrous foods in diet. Which might be from a number of things, but is usually from campers feeding animals soft and fatty foods.'

'Is it serious?'

'Can be. Weight loss and tiredness. Extreme infections over time will lead to death. You're looking at a possible significant impact on isolated populations, especially where that population might be stressed because of other factors.'

'So it's an animal welfare issue.'

'And a tourism issue, because the animals look awful and suffer, they have mouth and jaw swellings, their teeth are brown with tartar and they slobber and can't eat properly. So the public complains to Parks and Wildlife.'

'Interesting.'

Is it really, Evelyn thinks? Usually, people's eyes glaze over whenever she brings up lumpy jaw; sometimes her own do. She wants to turn back to the window, but sees he wants to keep talking, and it's probably good she learns a little about her colleagues. 'So have you always lived in Tasmania?'

'All my life. Love it, never want to leave, and particularly now I've got something important to fight for.'

'You mean the conservation movement.'

'The flooding of Lake Pedder back in 1972 was a tragedy but also a wake-up call. Just imagine, a beach of pure quartzite on a high inland lake, an amazing natural wonder, gone forever. But then I think because we lost Pedder, we were able to win Gordon-below-Franklin last year, stop them damming that magnificent wild river, with the present Hawke government's help of course. That first defeat gave us the focus and know-how. So now we must maintain the rage. Next big battle is the wood-chipping. Irreplaceable old growth sacrificed for easy money.'

'Well,' she replies, 'they tell us the eighties is supposed to be the greed is good decade. But then I wonder if it's ever been any different.'

'You know, when I was on campus in the late seventies, it was actually considered immoral to make money. I really think these last few years there's been a seismic shift in student attitudes. You must've come up against it.'

'Sydney's always been like that. What did you study at uni?'

'Same as you, zoology, but I see myself as a naturalist.'

'Meaning?'

'Someone who is interested in the natural world. I studied zoology because I couldn't think of anything else to do, but I also realised pretty early on it wasn't what I was about.'

'Too narrow?'

'Too focused. Any discipline like that leaves out far too much. I'm interested in animals, sure, but I'm more interested in the whole picture.'

'Sounds fine, but how do you find a living for yourself?'

'I don't know yet. But it seems to me you first work out what you want to do with your life, and then solve the problem of how to do it. Do you want your sandwiches?'

'Here, you take them. I'll just stick to the coffee.' She passes them back over and allows herself to return to the window.

They are flying slightly inland, hugging the south coast. Through breaks in the clouds, Evelyn watches glittering bays and muddy rivers silently scroll beneath as though they were part of some huge illuminated map, the shadow of the plane tracking like a ghost. Then thick white blocks all. The southerly change. The plane shudders and corrects.

Now there are two levels of cloud: an upper one that rushes by nervously, wraithlike; and a solid lower floor like a second earth with hills and valleys and plains but entirely white and bright, as if cleansed of all earthly stain, all toil and weakness and doubt, a fitting home for the gods. Here above her quotidian life, before it and after it, is this double world, gleaming pure in the sun, all the lovely silent spaces she has only dreamt of. It is too much and she turns back rubbing her face.

'Tired?'

Has he always got his eyes on her? Maybe just looking out the window himself.

'No, it's just that I haven't been in a plane for a while. I'd forgotten how extraordinary it is.'

'One of the few privileges of the modern world. A beauty for twentieth-century eyes.'

But he is not right, it seems to Evelyn, for philosophers and poets down the ages have described this world, if they have not literally seen it. Why does it hold such power for her? She's always been susceptible to physical beauty, an exception to one of her mother's many theories concerning the differentiation of the sexes. So Joseph has read her mother's books, and is an admirer of her mother's, admittedly admirable, public face. Janet Carter, anti-nuclear warrior and strident second-wave feminist. Fighting the good fight on many fronts. Yes, the macro is definitely in place, but what about the micro, what about the daughter for instance?

Although it's no big secret, Joseph could not know, because her mother never referred to it, that Janet Carter largely owed her freedom to roam the world and do what she pleased because of Evelyn's beloved father, Roy Carter, a successful property developer no less, white middle-aged male capitalist par excellence, dead of a stroke at his desk when Evelyn was six. Then Evelyn's mother, who as far as she was able to observe up to that point had been a quiet self-absorbed home-body, suddenly emerged as a glamorous seventies radical, lending her telegenic articulate presence to a range of leftist political and environmental causes, most particularly the nuclear disarmament movement, quickly becoming one of its international frontline spokespeople.

During that time, until Evelyn was twelve, she saw more of her mother's mother than her own mother. Gran moved into the family home to wash and cook and child-mind while her mother swooped in and out at will. Then she was placed in an expensive private girls' school, Frensham, up at Mittagong, where she boarded throughout the year. Each Christmas, Evelyn would fly to whatever exotic capital Janet Carter was holding court, New York, London, The Hague, and once, a very downbeat Moscow. There she would be smothered with kisses and gifts and introduced to her mother's latest high-profile beau, some of whom, in later years, were not averse to making the occasional pass at herself.

It was in her early teens that she missed her mother's presence most: lonely winter days listening to the highland rain patter on the large mossy flagstones of the school's central courtyard. She would sit hour after hour in an intense but undefined longing, fantasising, hoping, wishing, that her mother would suddenly march into the room and sweep her up in her arms and fly away with her. It was during that period that she found herself developing certain obsessional tendencies, for say, a piece of music heard on the radio, or a picture seen in an art book she had opened for no particular reason. The melody or the image could haunt her for months and she would find strange comfort in the indulgence. It was a kind of habit of mind that had remained with her, strengthened if anything, impacting unpredictably on her personal relationships.

She knew no boys until she attended Sydney University, and remained a virgin until that time. Not that sex itself had ever really been a fraught business for her, but relationships she continually obsessed about, not only boys, also her colleagues, her rivals, her supervisors. She had risen to her mother's unspoken challenge to become a brilliant, if somewhat reclusive, student. Her peers found her a bit daunting, but she was always respected.

Upon matriculating, her mother, then based in Paris, organised a generous monthly stipend, sufficient for Evelyn to manage her way through her degree. By that time, the family home no longer existed, and in many ways Evelyn still saw herself as being in her mother's hands. But she was determined to be independent, forge her own way. The last few times they had met, they had clashed, although it was difficult in retrospect to specify about what, since Evelyn basically agreed with most of her mother's views.

It did not help that Janet Carter seemed to take no particular pride in her daughter's academic successes. Maybe, Evelyn thought, it was simply what was expected. And surely, she could never have accepted her only child being an ordinary plodder, one of those plump, slow, always well-meaning girls Evelyn felt a strange sympathy for. People like that did not exist on her mother's radar, crammed, as it was, only with those individuals that mattered.

Also, being a 'great ideas' person, her mother had never either fully understood or accepted the importance of the concrete world for

Evelyn, how it had always intrigued her, and also helped anchor her. Plain evidence. Just that something is, herself included, had always for some reason seemed to Evelyn totally extraordinary, even miraculous. Which is why, she supposes, she finally became a scientist, and certainly why Nature is her big passion.

So then perhaps, she should be regarding this false landscape of clouds in scientific terms, not aesthetic or mystical. Here is an agglomeration of tiny water droplets randomly shaped by wind and temperature. That they are collectively beautiful and suggest to her a state of mind is perhaps irrelevant.

If she must interpret them as some kind of symbol, that symbol should also be scientific: that the world is knowable; given sufficient insight and resources, everything can eventually be explained. Surely that is her grail to seek, the scientist's, not the philosopher's or poet's. The light sculpting these shapes is one of rationality and optimism, and so also, for her, a kind of personal pledge that any phantoms that might beset her can be beaten with sufficient will and strength. And finally, that light seems to be telling her there can be no plurality of viewpoint: if the physical world is not objective and absolute, we are all lost.

'You sure you don't want anything to eat?'

Joseph's voice is strange, alien. Evelyn wrenches herself back to him.

'I'm not hungry.'

'The coffee's good, surprisingly.'

She swallows the last mouthful. He's right, it is good. It has given her a slight charge and she would like another cup. The stewardess is up front, bent over a passenger. She will try and catch her eye in a moment. She cannot think of anything to say to Joseph but he settles and closes his eyes.

'Is it possible to have another coffee?'

'Certainly, madam.'

Leaning across a now dozing Joseph, Evelyn suppresses an urge to take the pot herself and pour. She has always hated service, from both sides. However, this woman, smooth-faced, capable, a decade her senior at least, obviously doesn't mind the indignity, accepts it as part of the contract. Evelyn regards the crisp professional self-composure; a gulf separates her from this sister.

Outside now, close, dense cloud. She gulps down the scalding liquid, enjoying the intensity of heat and taste. There is a change of pitch in the white noise of the engines. Joseph stirs and Evelyn feels the cabin tip sharply. She looks at her watch. Descent.

Layers of cloud slide against each other in a shifting disharmony as the plane steadily cuts through. Suddenly Bass Strait is below, wild, cobalt and grey, white caps. They have left the land, the known; this is alien, frightening, but bracing too in a way. The colours are now all much colder. She shivers, and then the pain. She had forgotten how she always suffers upon descent. Hopefully it will not bring on a headache. Her temples throb. She mustn't show any sign of suffering to Joseph.

She turns further from him, jamming her face against the cold glazing. She will not be able to walk with one of her headaches. Now she can feel it at the back of her mind ready to pounce, then the wings dip as the plane quickly swoops in to land and she winces in agony at the toy houses of Devonport directly below. So close. She shuts her eyes, holds her breath. Just hang in there, another minute, too much. They bump down, a roar of deceleration, her ears pop in little sharp bursts but the big pain has retreated. Thank God. The plane drives towards a large barn that obviously serves as the airport. She manipulates her jaw to recover her hearing.

Devonport is chilly and overcast. It seems strange to Evelyn, these few houses and stores dwelling in this far-flung corner of the globe. They disembark and move out of the stiff wind into the single-roomed terminal. She stands next to Joseph; both wait for her luggage in slightly awkward silence. Finally it appears, on an open trailer pulled by an old jeep. The passengers must all go back outside and pick up their pieces from this trailer themselves. Evelyn looks around for a luggage trolley but there are none.

'My car's parked right outside,' Joseph says. 'Where are you staying?'

'I haven't booked anywhere. Thought I'd play it by ear.'

'Let me give you a lift into town to a hotel I know.' He cannot help but observe the pressure this places on her.

'No, I'll be all right.'

'Come on, it's only ten minutes out of my way.'

'Are you sure?'

'Sure I'm sure.'

'Okay. Thanks.'

'You right with your stuff?'

'Yes. I am.'

Pack on back and dragging her suitcase, she follows him out across the road to a rusty E.J. Holden station wagon. She has not seen a car of this vintage since she was a child. It has not been spruced up in any way.

'What are you looking at?'

'It's just that there aren't any cars like this left in Sydney.'

'Well, there's plenty in Tassie. You don't have to pass them over the pits for re-registration.'

The vehicle also appears as though it's never been washed. The back windscreen is plastered with sun-bleached conservation and Amnesty stickers, most notably the familiar triangular 'No Dams'. While Joseph digs his car keys out of the bottom of his pack, Evelyn notices the vehicle parked to the right, a large clean white utility with outsized new tyres. The sticker on its back windscreen reads, 'Update your fertiliser, plough in a Greenie'. The violence of this shocks her. Perhaps it's meant as a kind of rough joke. She is about to point it out to Joseph, but then decides not to.

He opens the boot and helps her stack her gear. 'Excuse the mess.'

The interior reminds Evelyn of a campsite before it's been struck: coils of rope, old clothes, tins of food, stained maps, even a rusted kero lamp.

'Hop in.'

Amazingly the engine starts first up; it must have been sitting out here for days, she thinks. Joseph seems unsurprised. He drives towards the centre of town at a leisurely pace, not bothering to indicate unless there is another car nearby and running a couple of orange lights, then suddenly he swings into the parking lot of a rather grand, Gothic-Victorian hotel.

'Here we are. You don't mind putting up at a pub, do you?'

'That's fine. I don't want to spend too much.'

'Good traditional comfort. Trust me. Haven't been here for a while, but nothing ever changes, which has its downside too of course. The owner's a cousin of mine.'

'A cousin?'

'Welcome to Tassie! Everyone's a cousin here,' he grins. 'Let me book you in.'

'No, please.'

'Let me do this one thing. Believe me, it helps you in these places if people can connect you to a local.'

No doubt he's right, she thinks. But also there is old-fashioned gallantry and chauvinism mixed up with it. Still, he has gone out of his way to give her a lift. It might look churlish and ungrateful to refuse his help.

'All right,' she agrees, 'since you're the local.'

Joseph moves around the back to get out her gear.

She jumps out after him. 'I want to carry my stuff!'

'Well, you take the pack. But at least let me take this suitcase.'

She remembers how heavy it had been at the airport. '…all right.'

'Christ!'

'Books and writing material. A few other odds and ends.'

Evelyn leads the way in. The corridor is empty and she rings the bell at the reception desk. After a while, a stocky middle-aged woman appears whose frosty mask melts immediately when she notices Joseph behind Evelyn. Yes, he is right; still it slightly rankles her.

'Hello, Kate!'

'Joey! Long time, no see.'

'Kate, this is Evelyn. She's heading up into the Walls tomorrow.'

'Well, we'd better make sure you're comfortable tonight, darling.'

'Can you organise a car for her and everything?'

'You can borrow the old ute if you want.'

'I'm happy to pay for it,' Evelyn breaks in.

'Well, we'll come to some arrangement.'

'I better get going,' says Joseph. 'No doubt I'll see you down in Hobart in a couple of weeks. I've still got a few things to tie up there before the big adventure, collecting gear and stuff, like you.'

'Thanks for everything. I mean it.'

'No worries. Good luck.'

She dumps her pack and they shake hands. Then, on an impulse, Evelyn follows him out of the hotel to wave. He toots as she watches his car chug up the dusty road. So relaxed, maybe it's just the men in Sydney, or the ones she meets. She'd wanted to be alone, but he didn't worry her. And what he said to her in the plane… She has studied hard and well, as no doubt he has, but this man, more or less her own age, she is certain knows far more than her about the natural world.

It is because the wilderness has always been his life and always will be. The presence, fact, of that huge virgin expanse must impact in some way, in many ways, on everyone's lives here. Vast untapped potential in a poor community. She has left Sydney and she is in a new place. She must try to understand it, if it is to be of value for her and her for it.

She stands a moment, then heavy rain, freezing, falls out of nowhere, forcing her reluctantly back into the foyer, where Kate is waiting patiently to sign her in.

First Entry

Her room is comfortable and sufficient, if a little cramped. On the glass-topped lowboy is a plastic-laminated combined Rules-of-the-House and Menu. Dinner is early, 5.30 to 6.30, and there are only two choices: Roast of the Day and Spaghetti Bolognese. So much for the vegetarians. It's now 4.30. Perhaps a pre-dinner gin and tonic. Evelyn walks downstairs and pokes her head in the public bar area. It is mostly full of men and warm and smoky and noisy, but the hum immediately abates as she is noticed standing in the half-opened door. For a moment, every eye in the room is fixed on her, then all turn back to their conversations, but at a slightly subdued level. She re-closes the door.

Back in her room, she sorts out her gear, then picks up the local newspaper, *The Examiner*, left on the one straight-backed chair. The paper is dated the previous week, not that that would make much difference, Evelyn reflects, as she flicks through. There is no international news, save the cricket, national news is confined to a domestic tragedy in Victoria and an anti-federal government diatribe by a local columnist, and the subject of this is the subject of virtually the entire paper: the forestry debate. And this 'debate' is no even-handed matter. What do all his 'cousins' think of Joseph's opinions, she wonders?

He certainly seems to have his battle cut out for him: 'The State Opposition joined a growing number of lobby groups in agreement with the State Government on the importance of the woodchip industry to Tasmania's economy.' On and on. She finds it all a bit dispiriting, not that it has anything to do with her; her interest here is confined to an existing National Park. But of course there are broader issues. Like dinner.

She retraces her way downstairs and through into the dining room which thankfully is empty, save for a farmer absorbed in a tractor manual, handsome, thirtyish, wearing an open-necked blue shirt, moleskins and R.M. Williams boots crossed casually at the ankle. He ignores her. She has a glass of local red with her roast, allows herself the trifle for dessert, and is just finishing with coffee when the farmer puts down his manual, rises and approaches. Here we go, she thinks.

'You must be Evelyn Carter.'

'How on earth do you know me?'

'Put two and two together. My name's Tony Warne. I'm the mayor. The council's putting a bit of money into your project.'

'Right. Well, that's good to know. So the council's interested in conservation.'

'Of course. We've got two of the state's major national parks on our doorstep.'

'Um, would you like to join me for a coffee?'

'Thanks, I've got to move on.'

'Sorry if I sound a little surprised. I've just been looking at the local paper upstairs. The community seems very pro-logging.'

'Pro-logging is not anti-conservation. Anyway, your work is in the park.'

'Of course. Are you involved in forestry?'

'No, I manage my wife's farm. But my great-grandfather milled timber from around this area after the fires of 1898. In the sixties, my father milled timber harvested from a forest that my brother is now harvesting again. No reason why it can't go on forever. Sustainable growth, Miss Carter, living with the land, using it. You ask Joseph Todd where the jobs are going to come from.'

'I will.'

'Nice to have met you. Good luck with your work.'

She watches him walk out with a lanky John Wayne gait. Just as well she is leaving tomorrow. Any longer and the whole town will know who she is, if they don't already.

After a sound sleep and a breakfast she would never have at home, bacon, sausages, fried eggs, stocking up on protein for the effort ahead, she strolls through the empty sunny streets to the local supermarket to supplement her supplies. It has rained briefly overnight and the morning is sharp, but the southern sky looks steady and clear. The girl at the checkout chats amiably while totalling her bill, a shopping novelty to her. She's feeling good, well fed and rested; Joseph's familial nudge was no scam. It seems that in this postmodern hi-tech world, certain country pubs still preserve their bottled goodness.

Then, for a payment of only one hundred dollars, Evelyn rents the pub's licensee's utility for apparently as long as she wants. She makes it clear she will need the vehicle for at least three months, probably four, although most of that time it will not be driven. She undertakes responsibility for all mechanical repairs, and all wear and tear and a full tank of petrol when she finally returns. All agreement is purely verbal, Joseph her unknowing guarantor.

She crams everything she can into the passenger side, secures the rest under a mouldy tarpaulin, then scans the map and heads off. Like Joseph's, the cold car starts first go, and once she gets the hang of the gears, responds superbly. It's such a delight to drive the solid make, lovingly maintained, despite odd patches of orange primer. She's away to a good start, so no need to hurry. For the first time in a long time, Evelyn feels herself uncoiling.

She idles mindlessly down quiet country roads, past tractors, mobs of cattle and sheep, through neat pocket towns with English and Gaelic and Aboriginal names, Barrington, Cethana, Parangana, past cultivated hills and fields, muscular countryside, rich warm browns and greens all bathing in the benediction of a bright morning sun. As the inland plateau area gradually nears, massive purple squat dolerite mounds and ranges rise in the distance and on either side. It is warming up now, rising air quivering through the windscreen, and the land appears unusually dry after the summer. Daydreaming, she narrowly avoids hitting an echidna, which suddenly shuffles out in front. She pulls over and pursues the animal into the bushes with her camera, but there is only a pair of strong hind legs kicking out comically under rubble. It has been a lucky escape for both as the echidna's strong spines are well-known tyre busters. As Evelyn recalls this, she also realises that she has never actually changed a tyre in her life.

Finally, she reaches the turn-off at the foot of the great plateau. Now the gradient steepens. She steers with care, and with considerable gear-crunching and bumping, along a succession of one-lane twisting dirt and gravel roads, probably unpassable in the wet. When the road seems about to thin into nothing, she squeezes past a series of small rock dams and comes to a clearing enclosed by a wall of brush. There are a few other cars and she seeks out a protective nook under a low tree, just in case of snow and wind. She knows the ranges are notoriously unpredictable.

The entrance to the park is clearly marked by the 'Warning' sign placed beside the track. Evelyn sidles out, stretches her legs with a few toe-taps and jogs over.

Walls of Jerusalem National Park. Fuel Stove Only Area. Do not enter park unless adequately prepared for extreme conditions. This is a wilderness area. There is no form of communication and no ranger. The plateau is very exposed and many walkers have been killed.

Very inviting. Beneath this is hammered a newer sign specifically relevant to Evelyn:

The Park will be closed from the end of February until the beginning of November for purposes of regeneration and scientific research.

A small pulse of pride.

She snacks, carefully assembles her pack, strapping on the aerial kit she has brought from Sydney, hoists it all, then locks up and sets off. From her detailed map of the park, she knows the first few hours walking will be toughest, the climb up onto the plateau, and then the going will be easier.

Under a strong afternoon sun, it is much harder than she expects up the steep narrow track, badly eroded, a tangle of roots and rocks, smell of ant and blossom and eucalypt, rush of steady breathing in her ears. Nectar-sipping rosellas, hanging upside-down from the blossoms, scatter haphazardly in brilliant flashes of colour at her approach. From the tops of the tallest trees flocks of yellow-tailed black cockatoos noisily protest her passing. It is muggy in this underbrush; sweat flows freely from under her hat and her back is quickly wet from the pack. Her shoulders protest, then settle and relax with her body heat, and her feet swell snugly into the old reliable boots.

It is so good to be walking at last after all the preparation and expectation, this job such an unexpected boon. Little more than two months ago there was only the prospect of dreary postgraduate study and here she is back in the wilderness.

She climbs out of the brush; the stately gums rise all around, varieties not visibly different to those Evelyn knows back in the Blue Mountains. As she ascends further, she observes how dark conifers increasingly dot the pervasive metal green, and she catches the occasional breath of icy air through the heat, like a sip of champagne.

Of course, this project is short and discrete. Unless it leads to something else, come mid-year she must again face the postponed decision on her doctorate. Well, she can shift cities, that is one thing, but does she really see herself as an academic? 'Work out what you want to do,' said Joseph. But that is so bound up with who you are. He seems to know himself, but she is still very much finding herself out, one of the many things she was hoping to achieve on this trip.

She toils an hour, then stops for a breather, leaning back against a mossy bank. A light plane drones high above, a toy drawn by string across a perfect arc of powder blue. And what does she look like from it? Something like the ants at her feet. As she strides over their trails, so she watches the plane quickly pass over her eventual goal. And what does that look like? Spectacular, no doubt. On the back of her park map is a pithy summary: 'Tasmania's Central Plateau rises abruptly 500 metres above the surrounding countryside. It was formed by a series of relatively recent volcanic intrusions and The Walls themselves are remnants of a higher plateau area. In the last Ice Age an ice cap of 65 kilometres in diameter covered the area.' So, by virtue of its height and isolation, there is nothing between the Walls and Antarctica but thousands of kilometres of wild cold air.

The Walls of Jerusalem. Now well settled into the rhythm of her climb, Evelyn forgets her body and contemplates this fabled landscape ahead. The 'double vision' of the clouds from the plane serves as a model. On one hand, she thinks, we have the 'poetic': pristine grandeur, impassivity, endurance, a metaphor for deity perhaps, indifferent, constant, containing immeasurable power and beauty; but then on the other, scientific knowledge and perspective gives an almost contrary reading. While the poet sees the eternal stasis, the scientist sees violence and turmoil, a place that has undergone great convulsion, recently, in terms of the Earth's history, so great it seems almost exhausted. But of course, the Earth is never still, nothing is still, and so the landscape will convulse again and again; it is actually in this process as she gazes upon it dreaming of fixity. Enormous forces, titanic energies are being expended, silently and ineluctably, and, it would appear, to no apparent end.

The scale and particularly the randomness disturb her. For she is also a part of this nature, but vitally different; a living organism with passion and independent will, imagined purpose, a miracle herself, to herself and, like every organism, for herself the centre of the world. Yet she is virtually nothing in this slow aleatory gigantism, passing sunlight on grass, dust to dust. To mean nothing, to be almost nothing, is beyond comprehension, since all that she is strains to expand into the world. Survival, at any cost, and for what? Well, to really reduce it to the scientific: reproduction's meaningless round.

At this thought, she sinks into mild depression, and then at once upbraids herself. How can she allow any downward drift at the start of such an extraordinary adventure? With this wonderful opportunity in hand, and with everything reasonably possible in life still stretching out ahead. She must drink up every drop.

Suddenly she trips over a large root, tumbling forward onto her hands and knees. Despite the weight of the pack, she is all right, just shocked and a little grazed. She rocks back on her haunches, straightens up, takes stock. She was not paying attention. Maybe she is pushing herself too hard and this is helping form negative thoughts.

Just ahead is a sharp bend with a view and convenient sandstone shelf to park a pack. Evelyn rests the bulk with relief, leans back and listens. You never hear it when you walk. A world without machines. A breeze sweeps across the valley and up to her with a sound that is subdued, but also profound, resonant. One can individually hear, as one can individually see when focusing, hundreds of thousands of trees responding in sympathy to its breath. Tuning in, she feels the society of the forest encompass her, the society of the wilderness. She is not alone. In fact, in a way she feels she is now entering her natural community, coming home.

Below and away to the left down a falling cadence of hills is the parking bay, scattered bright enamel tiles through the distant foliage. She looks for the ute but fails to find it; already she has climbed a good height, but above her the bush still seems to pile ever upwards. Jack and the beanstalk. She takes a long drink, counts slowly to thirty, shrugs back into her pack and presses on. She must not let herself cool and stiffen until she reaches the top. Pace herself, but maintain momentum.

Another ten minutes and she passes an old trapper's hut, crudely but soundly built, and resists the urge to again stop and rest. This shelter should mean she is near the end of the first stage, but the track just keeps looping up and up. Maybe she has taken the wrong trail. Impossible. She begins to tire, lose sense of how long she's been walking. It's all starting to look too much the same; maybe she isn't up to it, but she must be close now, she must, and if she's having these misgivings this early on, she cannot stop until she is sure she has reached the top. She tries to lose herself again in abstract thought, but her body insistently presses its discomforts upon her. At last, the gradient levels, and after a couple of hundred metres the forest thins, then opens out into a broad area of grassy marsh, unstable and studded with stagnant ponds.

Evelyn drops her pack, experiencing the forgotten strange release of this act as though gravity has suddenly diminished and some force is pulling her forward and up. Then she stretches her leg, arm and neck muscles, and pulls some chocolate out of one of the pack's side pockets. She washes it down with the last of the water she has brought from the hotel; it is bitter with heavy chlorine.

Someone has cleared this high ground in times past, possibly for mustering. Subsequent erosion will no doubt mean the path ahead is boggy and slow, but at least she's finished climbing. The few gum trees immediately around are all dead, some recently. From dieback? Marshy ground? She walks off the track a little, testing the firmness. Seems fine, but would probably turn to swamp with any rain. She's feeling better. The worst is over; this little rest and the prospect of easy going have revived her.

She presses on, trekking steadily across the flat ground, into the evening, gradually approaching the high area of the Walls, which themselves are now intermittently visible in the distance. Then, as though she is chance witness to some mystical or supernatural occurrence, the landscape slowly turns weird: light and form. Evelyn has seen this transformation previously in the highlands of Tasmania but has forgotten its intensity, although it is a thing walkers constantly refer to. Shallow snow pools lie on the large plateau in utterly still and limpid placidity, the general effect wrought to surreality by odd dead groves of gums, bone-white sentinels protruding starkly through the olive scrub. The land is silent, expectant; she feels like an intruder again. Surely this could not all be dieback. She knows that an horrific fire swept through in the early sixties. It's a fragile alpine environment.

Perhaps the gums simply have not regenerated. The less plentiful conifers seem unaffected.

Towards late afternoon, she comes to the site known as Solomon's Jewels, her planned stop for the night. From here she can clearly see the track up to Herod's Gate leading into the Walls beyond. The Jewels are an intertwined cluster of what her map titles 'tarns', small high-altitude lakes. They shine out luminously in the strange evening light. She finds a bare surface near the largest of them and pitches her tent, disturbing a big fat mother wombat with two cubs, which waddles off amiably into the bush. There are hours at her disposal with nothing for her to do but prepare dinner. The sky is still clear, the southerly latitude of the island making for long summer twilights, with the sun not setting until after nine and a general light lingering.

She fires her new gas stove, boils up rice and vegetables and fries some pork sausages bought that morning in Devonport, washing it all down with several cups of scalding black coffee. Then, employing her sleeping bag as a sort of outdoor couch, she settles back into the peace that follows hard physical exertion to enjoy the long twilight and dusk. From her position there is an untrammelled view right across the huge broad saddle and up the steep climb leading to Herod's Gate, which splits the Walls.

As the sun imperceptibly descends in the clear open sky, an uncanny red-gold glows from the hills and pools as though they are sources of light as well as the sun. In this heightened atmosphere, Evelyn can distinctly perceive every separate minute detail on the craggy massive cliffs of the pass she will climb through tomorrow. The extent and the precision of the detail, even more than the beautiful coppery light, give the scene a powerful otherworldliness. It appears a sort of 'super reality', just as she has seen rendered in the Romantic landscapes of Eugene Von Guérard in her home Art Gallery of NSW, never doubting the man to be extravagant and unbalanced by his own technical brilliance. Then, away from the gallery, one witnesses such a landscape in just such a way with the naked eye, the mind entirely composed and passive, purely receptive, unaided by any artificial stimulants or self-generated visions. There it is, just as fantastic as the canvases, not to be sensibly denied.

What would she be doing back in Sydney? What is Graeme doing? Working probably, making music. Part of her would like him here to share this, but a larger part of her is content to be alone. Beauty and love, such a commonplace association. She sees how she must resist the temptation to sentimentalise beauty, or allow it to sentimentalise her.

One of their last evenings together they had sat out in front of the Opera House, the summer air like a bath, watching the sun set under the bridge, its heat and light diffused by smog and low cloud. The harbour was raked with rose and gold, but for some reason it was all too much, either the lush and lurid loveliness of the view, or Graeme's cloying presence, or both. As the colours deepened, Evelyn had felt suffocated, almost nauseous. She had imagined tearing the vista right open with her bare hands, as though it were some glorious tapestry, ripping its gorgeous fabric to shreds to reveal something clear and clean behind, something fresh and new, something real. Maybe that was when she had decided to leave him, unconsciously, leave him and the clotted life she then saw before her.

This was before a concert he was to play; he was talented but not ambitious like her, content to be part of an ensemble. He looked so dashing in his tails. So Graeme will always have his music, his art to fall back on, and yes, she would like him here now, physically, his strong hands, his neat tense body. She liked him most after the concerts, shivering with the aftershock of performance, charged, needing her touch to release his pent-up passion. But you can't have that, and then just put it aside for something else when you please. The tangle of human relations.

She used to listen to the concerts equally compelled and irritated; compelled, sometimes overwhelmed, by the beauty of what she heard, irritated because she could divine no biological reason, meaning no real reason at all, for that beauty, unlike say, human physical beauty, which is obviously bound up in a complicated way with natural selection. One could make a rough analogy between the formal perfection of a Mozart concerto and a nautilus shell or a rose, but music could sometimes be formally perfect and also arid. What function did it serve? There was something vital here, some mystery that could not be explained, or not yet explained.

Her meditations are disturbed by a large, remarkably bold brush-tailed possum, striking silver-grey with black markings. It looks at her as at a long-lost companion, openly regarding her, like all campers presumably, as an easy source of dietary supplement, and she makes a mental note to fasten her food securely in the pack inside the tent.

Here is one native animal that has fared well from contact with man. Possums are great generalists, great adaptors. There were even a few living in the small park a block from Evelyn's flat in Alexandria, right in the heart of the city. This fellow is the biggest possum she has seen and she remembers now how possums and wombats are larger the more southerly the latitude, possibly because of the winters. She notes the naked patch just under the tip of the tail, which it basically uses as a fifth hand. So it seems she is not alone out here after all. And indeed, what other undeclared creatures of the wilderness might presently be aware of her? Joseph's mysterious dog, for example?

The possum settles close, up on its haunches, front paws raised in supplication. She ignores it, focusing her attention again on the view. Finally, the red-gold slowly fades to grey and shadows creep up the distant walls until only the serrated summits gleam. They too are swallowed by the dark, bringing a quickly deepening chill. Closer in, high in the air, a lone hawk still catches the sun, miraculously motionless save for a slight tense quiver, then plunges out of sight for a kill. Evelyn rouses herself with difficulty. She has stiffened up. She stretches, then tidies and settles to sleep.

The following morning is fine again, bright and sharp, the steely grain of the cliffs a different world to the previous evening. Frost sparkles on the rocks amongst the lichen, the early cold bites into eyes and skin. As she involuntarily braces against it, Evelyn is swept by an exhilaration perhaps not felt since childhood at the prospect of the spectacular morning's walk right up through Herod's Gate and beyond into the Walls. She has a light breakfast, quickly packs, and sets off.

The path winds through a small pencil pine forest stretching from the southern end of Solomon's Jewels, then bursts into the open plateau country and Evelyn can plainly see, much nearer now than from her camping spot, the ascent to the Gate. Coming suddenly out of the shadow of the trees, the high exposed saddle seems like a vast field of light. She moves as a tiny figure over an immense landscape, yet this morning she also feels that immensity within.

From her background reading, Evelyn knows the general windswept scrubby openness of the land to be not entirely natural. The Aboriginal inhabitants, long since killed off by white man's diseases and guns, used to regularly fire the forest and grasslands between October and March so that the hunters could circumvent and enclose their prey. Inevitably, the same tactics were used on them, as the wide plains they had created were useful for pasture and drew the Europeans. She notes there is no rainforest anywhere, unlike Cradle Mountain, Joseph's area, where she walked that student holiday. This land is too high and dry.

Crossing Wild Dog Creek, she refreshes her face with a numbing splash, then toils up the rise until finally she stands at Herod's Gate. She dumps her pack to rest and take stock.

Behind her, the white line of the track zigzags down and back through the huge expanse. Solomon's Jewels shimmer in the distance beyond the pine forest, and beyond them, she can see over to the lip of the great plateau. To its right, the immense bulk of Devil's Gullet, and to the left, even further in the distance, she thrills to recognise the fantastic purple peaks of the Cradle Mountain range, like old friends. Joseph is now presumably ensconced somewhere in there. And this, here, is her wilderness.

She turns back around. Ahead stand the Walls of Jerusalem. Immediately ahead, Lake Salome languidly stretches out its cerulean glitter under a cloudless sky, a small heaven itself, she thinks. A two-man yellow tent is pitched beside it towards this end, the first campers Evelyn has seen, although with the cars in the parking bay there must be others around. To her left, the impressive hump of Mount Ophel, scarred by the glaciers of the last Ice Age, and to her right, soaring straight up high above, the enormous Western Wall, the glory of the park, far too tall for the glaciers but sheered by them at its base, what geologists term a 'nunatak'. Beyond Lake Salome, the Temple Mount and Zion Hill, which hides from view majestic Mount Jerusalem, the tallest of the peaks. In its vast inert immensity, in the still warm midday, the landscape feels incredibly ancient, a land where the giants might truly have walked.

Evelyn pauses to absorb it, then pushes on through the Walls' alpine valley, through the clumps of tussock and snow grass and little communities of mat shrubberies and sedgeland. Particularly distinctive are the emerald green hemispheres of pincushion grass, spotlit against the graded olives of the other vegetation. She notes how all the shrubs have small heavily thickened leaves and tough flexible stems capable of surviving frequent snow and storms. The valley is generally too wide and exposed for tree growth, but odd sheltered areas harbour a few stunted pines and snow gums.

Occasionally she disturbs a small grey-green snake basking on the rocks, assuming it to be either a tiger snake or white-lipped whip snake. She knows both are poisonous, although it's very unusual for campers to be bitten by a snake; invariably they avoid you first. It is a reminder of how in so many ways she is exposed out here on her own. On her return trip, she will install a radio at the log cabin she is heading for, Dixon-Kingdom hut. She is carrying a first-aid kit and knows how to treat snakebite, but if she was well away from the hut, as she is now, and badly bitten, she could die.

Since the weather is holding, Evelyn postpones lunch until this destination, which lies outside the main area of the Walls, through Jaffa Gate and beyond an extensive forest of pencil pine. Dixon-Kingdom hut, when she returns to the Walls from Hobart in a month's time, when the park has been closed to the public, will be her home for three months. Like Joseph, her first short trip is an indulgence, to establish bearings and carry in notes, books, the aerial and a few luxuries she can secure in the metal cabinet of Joseph's key.

She labours slowly along the valley floor with the high peaks all around, feels especially the presence of the Western Wall rising immediately to her right. The path leads her to a scramble amongst the moraine rubble at its base, then a climb up to the saddle between the Western Wall and the Temple Mount, known as Damascus Gate.

From here, Evelyn looks over into yet another world, over the largest surviving forest of pencil pine in Tasmania, and down the long valley to Lake Ball. On the haze of the horizon, she dimly discerns the crooked peak of Frenchman's Cap in the south-western ranges. While descending towards the fringe of the pines, the end mass of the Western Wall, Solomon's Throne, suddenly blocks her sun. The shadow is surprisingly cold. She turns back to regard the cliff. The silhouetted bulkhead seems strangely threatening. She puts her back to it and plunges into the forest.

The trick in moving through the woods so that she will emerge near the hut is, more or less, to maintain contour and resist descending into the marsh skirting Lake Ball. The forest of pencil pines is straight from a children's fantasy, Grimm or Tolkien, the venerable trees, thousands of years old in some cases, wonderfully twisted by age and extreme weather, their stationary shapes speaking clearly, eloquently, of the violence they have endured. Now one could almost worship them like a druid. Between the trunks, fresh clean grass, neatly clipped as though by some mower, the result of natural gardeners, wallabies and kin; and as this thought occurs to Evelyn, she happens into a small clearing and the freshly killed remains of a pademelon. Bones and skin are scattered widely. Not the work of the scavenger cat-like Tasmanian devils, which would leave nothing. And the animal's neck appears to have been broken.

She drops her pack. Also the scats are too large for devils, like those of a big dog. The pademelon has been killed by the dog that over-excited campers have reported as a thylacine. So, it looks like she is sharing her new home with a feral, which she reflects, must have travelled a considerable distance. There aren't any farms for hundreds of kilometres and the terrain is very difficult. There are no dingos in Tasmania, no native dogs. Such a pity that introduced beasts can penetrate so deeply into wilderness. She'll report it back in Hobart. As Joseph said, if there is a dog in the area killing the wildlife, somehow it will have to be caught and perhaps destroyed.

She continues and in another fifteen minutes spies the hut at the edge of the woods. It is almost too picturesque, distinctly European with the firs backing. At first glance it seems in excellent repair. Built by Reg Dixon, she has read, an itinerant who first came up into the area in the 1930s when the Depression pushed labourers into trapping here despite the wretched conditions. Animals in the highlands were always favoured, as their pelts were thicker. Possum skins from here sold at twenty-five shillings each, a lot of money at the time.

She circumnavigates, admiring the engineering. To build the hut, Dixon dragged logs to the site by horse and levered the timber into position. Fallen pencil pines were split into shingles, stacked to dry, then laid on the roof the following year. Evelyn knows this much about Dixon as he also has a minor zoological claim to fame. On one of his many excursions here, in the 1940s when he was trying to acclimatise some cattle, Dixon sighted a mature Tasmanian tiger, by then declared extinct.

The walls of the cabin are thick logs stacked one on top of the other, weathered to a silvery sheen. She is astonished at one man and a horse accurately shifting and fitting such weights. Inside, it is damp and musty, but habitable, even homely. There is one glass window and an efficient fireplace with a soot-clear flue. Flagstones have been set on the floor, and against the wall opposite the hearth is a wooden ledge that could sleep about five. Next to this is a small door leading to an enclosed, newly installed, chemical pit toilet annexed to the back, courtesy of National Parks, and the necessary equipment needed to keep it in good order. Another recent addition is the heavy metal cabinet sitting squarely to one side, and above it some shelving. There is even a small crude desk near the fireplace, glazed with accreted candle wax. Apparently, there are no campers in residence, but much graffiti, candle butts and horror tales in the logbook show the hut is well patronised.

Miraculously, the key smoothly works the cabinet lock. Evelyn unpacks and neatly stores her books and notes inside with some other pieces. She'll erect the aerial tomorrow; it's no use without the radio, but she should locate the drop Joseph mentioned.

After some aimless wandering, she finds it behind a boulder about fifty metres up the valley. It doesn't appear to have hit the rock, and the traps and bundles of food seem fine. She lugs all this back and, after checking it all carefully, stows it under the wooden 'bed'. There is no food for herself, only what she will need to start her work: plentiful apples, and peanut butter and vanilla essence to smother them with. Macropod manna. What next? There is still plenty of daylight left; the light seems to last forever up here at the end of the world. So, maybe a swim in Lake Ball.

She strolls down the valley and seeks out a firm spit of land from which she might easily enter the water. At her feet, the whisper of the waves is an intimate self-sustaining monologue, interrupted by the occasional bird disturbed by her presence, flapping up feverishly out of the marsh weeds. As they rise, their little cries etch the silence. Farther out, the surface appears perfectly still. Brown fuzzy patches of gnats hover at irregular intervals.

These high-altitude lakes seem to her epitomes of the wilderness itself, wells of purity, 'great crystals on the surface of the earth' as Thoreau described them. She quickly strips, plunges in and is at once stunned by the cold, but then how wonderful to feel the sweat streaming from the body, to be cleansed by the wilderness. She breaks surface, catches breath, and strokes out to the centre. Her body feels heavier than in the salt sea with which she is familiar. It looks to her so white, so pampered and civilised, almost insubstantial. The splintered light on the surface from the low sun dazzles. Evelyn stretches back, arms out, looking up into the deep blue zenith of the sky, and for an instant her mind opens, transparent to the high clarity above.

Back at the hut, she sits out on a weathered log, staring down the valley in the sunshine as the afternoon shadows slowly lengthen, down the broad vista that sweeps away to the peaks of the south-west ranges, staring in solitude and a sort of waking sleep until the cold finally overtakes her and she rouses herself for dinner. She cannot remember ever being so relaxed and content. Now a few clouds, high and large and flat, hang lazily in the south-west. They seem motionless, to have been painted onto the pale blue dome of the sky for a little variety and decoration, as in a baroque cathedral.

However, half an hour later when she glances up from her cooking, the clouds have increased significantly in bulk and number. Curiously they still look static. There is such a complete contrast in texture between the thick white bunched cauliflower formations and the empty clean sky, now slowly turning translucent in the evening. In the distance under the largest cauliflower she observes storms over Frenchman's Cap, and also different flat clouds moving quickly towards her. Approaching bad weather at least means a fine sunset.

She tidies up, leaving unwashed plates and cutlery outside, so possums won't be encouraged to enter the hut. Then walks out, disturbing some Bennett's wallabies and pademelons, which have silently, unobtrusively appeared with the dusk. They are curious of her but keep their distance.

The same strange red-gold colour of the previous evening again highlights the magnificent crinkled surface of the cliffs, and also lights the bunched clouds, initially in a sharp yellow-gold, which gradually turns pink as the sun descends. Silent passion. The flat clouds have thinned, dissolved; as her eye traces their threads to nowhere, an immense calm possesses her, the calm of the great glowing evening itself seems to cup her. Except that on the horizon are mute disturbing flashes of lightning, and minutes later, dim, seemingly unconnected, drum rolls of thunder.

Finally, the spectacle darkens to the colour of the night sky and Evelyn turns in. Too happily excited to sleep, she lies on her back listening to the cracking of the wood of the hut as the cold contracts it, peering through the gloom at the uneven rafters which are like a second skin between her and the wilderness. They provide vital protection, but she can still feel the outside through their membrane.

She sleeps and wakes prematurely. A wind is howling up the valley, an enormous extraordinary sound. The wild is no longer friendly, but huge and incomprehensible. She drifts into uneasy dreams, haunted by the wind.

Suddenly she is sitting up; all of her senses have jarred together. She shakes her head, feeling odd, not good. She will step outside, clear her mind. She pulls on her parka.

It is very cold, much colder than she expected. Strangely, it is not windy, but she can still hear it, hollow and weird; this particular valley must be sheltered from it. The wallabies have all disappeared. She tries a few hesitant steps through the dewy grass, tense, alert.

Where is this strange silver light coming from? Evelyn looks up and gasps. Somehow she has forgotten this since her last field trip, the stars in the bush, how much the city dulls their splendour, this lavish spangled profusion of icy worlds scattered across the vast night sky with a seemingly voluptuous negligence. She feels giddy, not as if she is looking up, but if she were looking down, into some bottomless lake. Chaos, and yet so beautiful. She should learn something about the stars, or would that reduce them, or simply give the false impression of reducing them? For how could you possibly reduce this? How could you ever possibly grasp it? As scientists, as poets, as lovers, we impose our meaning upon them, but then their own meaning flows so eloquently back to us. And of course, she thinks, our dominating life-sustainer, our sun, maybe life-creator, is just another slowly cooling star amongst these expanding infinitudes.

There is a movement to her right, near the bushes where her cutlery is. A possum, or maybe native cat. She stares over at the area but can make out nothing in the dark. She returns to the glory above: God's diamonds, the floor of heaven. The wind picks up, piercing her parka and thermals. She must return to the hut before she chills.

A loud rustle and the distinct rattle of cutlery. She starts towards the noise to frighten the creature, but stops in her tracks at the dim sight of, yes, a large dog steadily observing her from the shadow beyond the bushes at the edge of the forest. The killer of the pademelon, unless there are more than one. It watches her, then slinks with an odd gait back into the trees. She stares at where it has vanished. In her surprise she has hardly seen it at all. That funny gait. Perhaps it is carrying an old injury.

Evelyn stands transfixed and an irrational fear steals over her, a fear without source or meaning. She is spellbound by some primitive spirit of the wilderness, alone and vulnerable in the cold night, the indifferent stars glittering above. Why is she so tense? Why is she thinking like this? A few bad dreams. She must get a hold of herself. Not moving, she looks carefully around, but can see nothing unusual. And that is because there is nothing unusual. Except that dog. Has it gone away? It's only interested in food scraps.

Shivering now, she returns to the hut, and for peace of mind, although she knows it is silly, fixes the heavy wooden door firmly in place with a solid rock from the fireplace. Leaving her parka on, she wraps herself in the sleeping bag, and eventually the excessive warmth spreads through her body and drugs her back to sleep.

Next morning, the clouds of the previous evening have blown over and again it is fine. Evelyn must be in Hobart by the following evening, but with the weather miraculously holding and virtually no weight on her back, there is ample time to explore as long as she reaches the car before dark.

The day proves the climax to a sequence of exhilarating days. The positive intense wildness of the landscape is now fully internalised; a lid has lifted off the world for her.

She constructs and erects the aerial, securing it to the chimney, then gathers her gear and heads off. First, she dumps her pack and scrambles to the summit of Mount Jerusalem. From here she can see the grey pitiless wasteland of tarns and rocks and dead gums that stretch south towards the Great Pine Tier. Impossible country, summer or winter. Round to the east are the forested lakes, evergreen and blue like a postcard from the Swiss Alps. Their orientation is either north-west or north-east, the directions of the fault lines of the plateau where the ice cap has gouged. On large exposed rocks are streaks of rust, ironstone country where compasses are useless. Above, a pair of wedge-tailed eagles circle lazily on the thermals, a juvenile and an adult, she thinks. The Walls would be an ideal nesting area for these superb raptors.

Descent, her pack, and back off towards the central area of the Walls leading eventually to the long downhill track past Solomon's Jewels and to the car. En route she conquers King David's Peak. As she picks her way up the steep scree and gingerly edges around piled-up dolerite boulders, twinges of a headache unexpectedly appear, a little throbbing at the temples, and her mind starts to cloud, but it disperses when she reaches the summit and relaxes with the view. She waits until her eyes adjust to the glare. A quick flicker of hawk-shadow, such a contrast between light and dark in this high cool dry air. Another flicker: a small skink, basking invisibly, slips silently into a crevice of a smooth and weathered boulder right at the very lip.

From this peak, Evelyn can see the whole of the walk back to where the car is hidden over the edge of the great plateau. The foreshortening astonishes. All that distance she has toiled and must still toil.

Solomon's Jewels look truly like small gems. Only from an aspect as this can one really gauge man's proper size, realise his view of his own greatness derives from a blinkered vision. Again the descent, and in a few hours' quick downhill stride, she is back at the car park.

Driving back to Devonport, the weather closes in with the dark. It is as though the sun has shone only on the Walls. In her two previous trips to Tasmania, Evelyn has never known such fine weather at a stretch, particularly on the highlands. In retrospect, her little preparatory trek appears above all incredibly bright; actual shards of it seem to be lodged in her corneas, glowing palimpsests on the dark winding road ahead. Largely, she supposes, this is because she has been spending the full extent of long days out in the open, in high valleys and on mountain peaks with vast expanses of wilderness, often reaching to the limits of the horizon as far as the eye can see, and consequently with a greater sky vaulted over.

But also the light itself has seemed more intense, of greater clarity, possibly because of the altitude, and conversely she supposes, because of the quantity of dust and dirt she is accustomed to in Sydney. She has absorbed such an excess of concentrated light, such density of the stuff, she feels she will carry it around in her head for weeks. *Lux aeterna.*

That night, back in the pub in Devonport, Evelyn closes her eyes in the dim little room to return to a huge other-world of bright and spectacular beauty, an involuntary internal projection of what she has ingested. So tomorrow she will arrive at Hobart with sun-flushed face and arms and a pink peeling nose, more than a little sun-struck. Because it has all been more than wonderful, more than she could possibly have expected. Her eyes are shut tight, but the eye of her mind has briefly dilated.

Hobart

'You have that in Sydney?

A bird like a plump sooty seagull preens itself on the scalloped zinc surface of an empty table next to theirs, keeping an eye out for scraps.

'No. Muttonbird, isn't it?'

'Otherwise known as the short-tailed shearwater. *Puffinus tenuirostris*. Each season, that bird makes a migratory round trip of thirty thousand kilometres all the way up to the Bering Sea and back here to exactly the same burrow.'

So wherever it is in the world, Evelyn thinks, it knows its home. It's a kind of miracle, that's what the professor is implying, that they both share and know through their discipline, that tiny heart beating in faith through unimaginable adversity. Evelyn watches her mentor stretch back, fingers interlocked, and gaze up at the bright depthless blue.

'When I was a boy, my father used to take me to the beaches with him to collect the eggs. The mother protects them in a long hole. Occasionally a snake will find them and curl up for an after-dinner nap. When you reached into that hole, you were never too sure what you would find.'

'Do people eat them?'

'They were a staple diet for the Aborigines. Poor people too. We did.'

Evelyn has spoken and corresponded with Professor Atherton at length, but never met him. For some reason, she had formed a mental picture of him as chubby and balding, slightly frayed at the edges, dandruff and cigarette ash. In fact, he is small and slight, compact, well preserved for a man in his sixties, a dignified patrician with a full head of silver hair. Even on Saturday morning, he is wearing a dark suit and college tie.

'I must tell you, professor, that I wrote an essay on your monograph on the platypus in my first undergraduate year. I found it fascinating.'

'Thanks. It's because the creature itself is so fascinating. When the first specimen was sent back to London, the scientists thought it was a fake. Darwin was particularly taken by it, as you can imagine. Did you know Darwin stopped in Hobart during his voyage on *The Beagle*? He did a walking tour of the Eastern Shore and also climbed Mount Wellington. He might very well have sat where you are now.'

She smiles at the thought. Charles Darwin, a hero of hers, as the professor well knows. They are sipping coffee at the weekly Salamanca Place markets, obviously a popular gathering spot for the city. For their first meeting, the professor has kindly offered to show Evelyn some of the tourist sights.

It has been a leisurely and enjoyable morning. On the whole, the stalls here seem to her far less trashy than like markets in Sydney. There are bargains even, particularly among the booksellers. And unusual items: beautiful shells collected locally, of an abundance, size and variety that must have once graced her own local beaches; intricate woodworkings from the regional timbers; spectacular wilderness photography; skilled landscape oils and watercolours; all manner of home-made jams and preserves.

'You met Joseph on the plane as arranged? He should be about somewhere. He works on the Wilderness Society's stall. Can't see them.'

Evelyn looks around. It is mostly a young crowd, yuppies and greenies dominating the bric-a-brac. Those she expects, but is surprised to find the greenies merging indiscernibly into a sizeable population of hippies, genuine, straight from the sixties, not the mid-forty gentrified species still extant in Sydney's Paddington. In the hard-edged rationalist gelled silver-and-black eighties, here are young people in cords, flannelettes, beads, long hair, squatting by a stone wall in the sun, obviously an habitual territory, reading tarot or playing flute, recorder, guitar for a bit of bread. Forgetting the rat race and getting back to nature. However, they don't look to her as if they could actually survive in the wilderness, unlike Joseph Todd. Rather, that they have adapted to city life, like some new breed of domesticated marsupial.

'Do you still teach zoology, professor?'

'Not much. I'm based at the School of Geography and Environmental Studies.'

'Actually, I ran past your building this morning.'

She had risen early and jogged out far along the bay, looping back through the grounds of the university. She'd settled quickly into a good rhythm; the air was crisp, tart, wonderful. While she is here preparing the outlines of her research with the professor, Evelyn is determined to improve her fitness, so that she can handle field studies in the severe weather she knows she will encounter leading into winter.

Professor Atherton is the originator and overseer for the entire wilderness project. Four National Parks have been temporarily closed, with resident scientists studying various adverse impacts of public access on wildlife and landscape. The other two are environmental biologists, older than her and Joseph by a decade. Evelyn has not met them and will not. They are already in their specified areas gathering data and compiling their reports.

Despite Evelyn's lack of experience in remote area work, she assumes she has been invited to participate in the project, at the last minute apparently, because of the relevance of her Honours thesis, which examined differing long-term effects of white settlement on the wildlife of the Blue Mountains behind Sydney.

Although, she is now thinking, the Walls have no rural residential development. There may be some pollution in the waterways and minor firewood collection issues, but the Blue Mountains have been built on, walked over, mined and periodically settled for centuries. Whereas the Walls of Jerusalem is a wilderness, pristine, although presumably the lumpy jaw she is to examine is mostly coming from the campers. Nevertheless, what she does feel strongly, particularly this morning chatting casually to the professor, is that if her work over the ensuing months is to be at all useful, she must try and understand the manifold ways in which the Walls differ from anything she has previously known.

'Professor, what do you hope to achieve from this project?'

'You do know that it's part of a wider political agenda.'

'No.'

'Everything concerning conservation is political down here.'

'I'm starting to grasp that.'

'Well, leaving to one side the intrinsically valuable information all of you will glean, broadly, my department and the Greens hope to use the results of the studies to lobby the state and federal governments for more funding for the parks. Every year we get more visitors into these areas. That is good, of course, but as you know, inevitably they degrade wherever they go, to say nothing of the various impacts on the wildlife, such as lumpy jaw. So we need to repair past damage, maintain tracks and campsites, maybe even restrict numbers if there are serious problems, or if the money is not forthcoming. With public attention still focused on the Greens after the Gordon-below-Franklin victory, now is the time to move.'

'You think conservation will go off the boil?'

'It's probably already happening. Politicians have short memories, part of their Darwinian survival kit.'

Evelyn looks askance at the professor; he seems an unlikely greenie. Then she experiences a déjà vu: Joseph is running up through the crowds towards them in the same exuberant manner that he ran for the plane, and despite the chilly wind he is wearing the same Wilderness Society T-shirt. It strikes her how comfortable and easy he is in his body. He pumps the professor's hand, but this is not sufficient, so gives him an awkward bear hug and even a small kiss on the cheek. Obviously, they are close.

He soberly shakes Evelyn's hand, the grip still uncertain. 'How are you going, Evelyn?'

'Okay.'

'Enjoying the Walls?'

'Very much.'

'I've got to tell you I've just read your paper and how much I enjoyed it.'

'What!'

'The prof lent it to me. Hope you don't mind. It's great to have people like you working for us.'

'You read my thesis?'

'As I said, Evelyn,' the professor cut in, 'conservation is serious business down here. We're not just city sympathisers. Joseph was arrested during one of the blockades in the Franklin campaign. So was I.'

'Not in your suit, I hope.'

'As a matter of fact, yes.'

'Made excellent copy,' smiles Joseph. He pulls over a seat. 'When did you get here?'

'Yesterday. I drove down in your cousin's ute.'

After all her outdoor exertion, Evelyn had uncharacteristically enjoyed the enforced dull relaxation of the day drive down to Hobart. While it had not rained on the highlands, it obviously had recently in the east, for she could not recall ever seeing country so vividly green. A green and pleasant land, just as she had imagined England from its literature. The neat Georgian townships along the way had conspired with the fantasy, quaint and historic, cool and contained. Between the towns, lush, rolling hills had seemed to spread out forever beside an empty road.

'Where are you staying?'

'With an aunt of my mother's, Amy Meadows.'

'The landscape painter,' says the professor.

'You know her.'

'Everyone over a certain age knows everyone else over a certain age in Hobart,' smiles Joseph.

'My wife's a bit of an art buff. It's good if you can stay with a local.'

More or less what Joseph had said to her.

Evelyn had reached the city late afternoon, a dusty honeycomb glow still lingering in the air, materialised in the old sandstone public buildings. A weekday, but compared to Sydney there was no traffic; she easily worked her way through the centre and south towards Amy's suburb.

The house proved rather grand, a battleaxe block approached by a long, steep drive past two humbler dwellings beneath. Thinking it unwise to test the ute on the incline, Evelyn parked, and ascended on foot. At her tentative knock, the door opened at once as though Amy Meadows had been waiting and watching for hours.

Amy wore corked platforms that Evelyn dimly remembered from girlhood in the early seventies, thick harlequin woollen stockings, a pleated purple skirt with non-matching patches, and an old ribbed mustard jumper partially but not mercifully covered by a paisley green vest. The ensemble was triumphantly crowned with a wide-brimmed battered straw hat with dried native flowers jammed in the band.

Apple-cheeked Amy cradled a tiny kitten with sealed eyes, which mewed blissfully. Without any word or preamble, she leaned stiffly forward and planted a big wet moustache-tipped kiss on her great niece's pursed lips. The kitten emitted a plaintively jealous cry.

'Isn't it a darling? One of only three left. The rest of the litter had perished. I've taken them all in of course, and mama. What else could I do? I've named them after the three graces. This is Euphrosyne.'

'What have you called mama?'

'Tabby. Actually she's black and white. Don't just stand there in the wind, dear. Come in. Is that all your luggage?'

'A few bits and pieces in the car. I don't have much.'

'My make-up kit's bigger than that. Yes, it's terrible these poor mothers dying in the cold. Someone should go around and shoot the toms.'

'She must have been party to the process.'

'Goodness! What a thought! Must be the scientist in you.'

The house was a shambles: cat hair, odd easels, half-completed bushland scenes, paintbrushes, turps bottles, rags. Oils and sketches seemed to cover every square inch of wall. Above the fireplace was a grand romantic landscape of the Derwent River and Mount Wellington, slightly smoke-damaged, which might have been a Haughton-Forrest.

'Didn't do that one unfortunately, dearie. Old sea captain. Caught the bay perfectly. See.'

With a flourish, Amy threw back the curtains, revealing a broad late-light sweep of the Derwent River. Evelyn gasped at the sudden stunning vista.

'I save it for special occasions.' She drew the curtains shut. 'Like a cuppa?'

'Thank you.'

'Only have herbals.'

'Fine.'

'Be a jiffy.'

Evelyn perched on the edge of one of the furry armchairs and at once a marmalade monster was on her lap. She stroked the beauty, which arched proudly, twitched a flagpole tail, purred machine-like, circled three times, pricked her jeans and settled down permanently. Most of her zoological comrades disliked cats, seeing them simply as feral pests, but Evelyn loved all animals. This friendly fellow could hardly be expected to know he really should not be here, and in fact he looked very much at home, as did they all. A few weeks with Amy and her feline family would no doubt prove diverting.

She is brought back to the markets.

Joseph has been in intense conversation with the professor. Local politics. Now he turns a serious face to Evelyn to include her, 'The thing is we've finally got the Greens' leader, Bob Brown, in parliament, and everyone's hoping the issues can be fought in a more civilised fashion. I really believe the public and the press are slowly moving behind us.'

'Both arrested. I thought you were all heroes at the time,' Evelyn says wistfully. 'I wanted to run away from school and join you.'

'But you have your heroes up in Sydney too. Jack Mundy, the trade unionist who saved all those historic buildings, he's a great man.'

'He is, but everyone's forgotten it now. Black-banned and on the dole. Unbelievable! Nobody cares in Sydney.'

Joseph is again struck by her bitterness. He watches her shift restlessly in her seat.

'Joseph,' says the professor, 'do you want to join us for some lunch?'

'I'm on the stall. I should be there now. But I could manage dinner.'

'Even better. My wife can join us for a foursome. All right with you, Evelyn?'

'Sounds fine.'

'I'll organise it and pick you up at about six.'

'Sure. Thanks.'

'I'd better get back,' says Joseph.

Evelyn watches as his figure merges back into the crowd. Everything is bright and vibrant in the clean cold light, and as she gazes beyond the bustle, along the perspective of convict-hewn storage buildings with their faded kitsch Victorian advertisements, her eye is drawn up naturally, like the artist over Amy's fireplace, to the dominating bulk of Mount Wellington, next stop on the professor's tour, at present swathed in a cloak of shaggy dark cloud. Majestic solitude and masculine melancholy. Yes, the wilderness is always a definite presence here, even when one is amongst the 'throng' of the capital.

Professor Atherton and his wife are punctual for dinner. Evelyn is not ready and has to leave the couple to Amy while she blows her hair and irons an outfit. Fortunately, Mrs Atherton can discuss Tasmanian art and artists, but Evelyn is unhappy at them speaking to Amy, and so is put out more than anyone by her own lateness. The reason she feels this way, although she knows it is irrational, is because of a conversation over tea and scones with her great aunt that afternoon:

'I can see,' Evelyn had said, with Joseph's morning words in mind, 'that

I'm going to have to get a firmer grip on the background issues here, the conservation movement, the Greens and Bob Brown, all that.'

'Non-violent resistance,' replied Amy, 'that's what he preaches, my dear, inspired by Gandhi apparently, and it's worked. They even had training camps at one stage. I considered attending, but couldn't leave my cats. You might or might not have noticed, but we're very idealistic down here.'

'Yes. Even the farmers it seems, although all the idealisms don't necessarily mesh.'

'I do believe people like Bob Brown, and also your mother incidentally, can actually change the world.'

'My mother?'

'People care, both ways. Don't imagine they don't. Do you know that Janet regularly gets death threats through the mail?'

'No, no, I did not know that!'

'Don't want to sound too alarmist. Nothing's ever happened. She's sure it's merely standard CIA scare tactics. But your mum's hot, darling. Larger than life. And your Professor Atherton's a great admirer too.'

'He hasn't mentioned her to me.'

'Last year he published a long essay in *Island* magazine about her international impact on the environmental movement. I've probably still got it around somewhere. Funny he hasn't referred to it.'

Not funny, thinks Evelyn; an intentional omission. Why? Because he worries she might think he has chosen her partly because of her mother? Or because that is the case.

'You should bring it up with him.'

'To be completely honest with you. Amy, my mother and I aren't that close. Not that I don't admire her work.'

'Does she embarrass you?'

'Not exactly.'

'Public persona and mother not such a good fit, is that it?'

'More or less, I suppose.'

'Evelyn, how can I describe it to you? Your mother is living out a kind of opera. It's grand and it's beautiful. It's difficult for you, naturally, but the work she is doing is essential. I'm sure in time you will come to see her like the rest of us.'

'Perhaps. I hope so.'

'To be a prophet is always problematic, particularly for those closest.'

'It's just that I could have used a little more personal support over the years, that's all.'

'So could have we all.'

'Amy, my mother never doubts. Can you imagine that?'

'Surely it's a strength.'

'Everything she does is justified.'

'But perhaps it is.'

'Her optimism and her anger seem, I don't know, relentless.'

'Partly a defence mechanism. Her father beat her and her brother black and blue quite regularly. Did you know your grandfather?'

'He died before I was born.'

'Thank God the grog finally killed him. I can say it. He was my brother after all. To survive with a parent like that, you either come out hard and strong, or you go under. Ted, your uncle, went under.'

'Yes, I know. I might go for a run.'

'On those scones?'

'A walk. See you in a little while.'

Now she is sitting irritably in the back of the professor's car, an ancient Morris, picking at a loose edge of vinyl, unable to make conversation until her present mood passes. She wants to enjoy the evening, but needs something external to lift her. She watches listlessly out the window at the neat suburban cottages passing, one after another.

When they arrive, Joseph is at the bar enjoying a quiet beer. Evelyn enviously observes his solitary self-possession, then he turns and gives her a big wide open smile, and at once she relaxes.

It is a Thai family business, all close and friendly. The delicious aroma of spices also helps settle her. They are seated at a table with a fine view of the river. It is a cloudless night and a crescent moon has just pulled clear from the dark flat headlands.

'Hobart is such a pretty place,' Evelyn remarks dreamily, looking out the window.

'Then you're well suited for it, my dear,' replies the professor.

This causes Evelyn a return burst of irritation she suppresses with difficulty. He is only being old-world polite, she knows, but she hates compliments, particularly physical compliments, which to her invariably suggest a disregard for person. Would he have said such a thing to her mother? On her side, she has a private rule never to physically compliment a man, least of all a boyfriend. And certainly it seems they have needed no encouragement.

Joseph notices the look of intensity on her face prompted by the professor's comment and wonders at it. He says, 'Nice to be able to live in a city with nature all around.'

'Yes,' she replies distractedly, returning to the window. As she gazes, she feels the view entering her, almost against her will. 'I find nature, wilderness, very powerful at times, sometimes too much.'

She is speaking half to herself. Her eyes shine and Joseph sees how important the moment of experience is for her. Perhaps it is everything. This is a scientist, but no dry rationalist. For this woman, something is either a passion, or it is nothing. Watching her watching the scenery, the strange thought then occurs to him that it's almost as if she has some element of the wilderness within her.

'Well,' he says, again filling up the gap, 'we'll both be out in it on our own shortly.' Did this sound inane? It is a bit difficult to be natural with her.

'I'm sorry you have to be on your own,' says the professor. 'I had hoped to send in teams, two or three, but we just didn't have the money.'

The waiter now returns and exchanges a few friendly words with the Athertons. Menus always throw Evelyn into a quandary. This is clearly a favourite restaurant of the professor's but she wants to avoid asking his advice, and particularly in front of the waiter.

'What kind of wine are you thinking of ordering?' she asks him.

'What would you like?'

'A red, if that's all right with everyone.'

'I'll stick to beer,' says Joseph.

'Mary?' asks the professor.

'Red's fine.'

'Red it is then,' he smiles at Evelyn.

She returns to the menu. Red helps narrow it a bit. Maybe seafood would have been a better idea; she never cooks it herself.

The waiter is hovering behind and she makes a sudden decision on the jungle curry.

'That is hot, madam.'

'That's okay.'

He takes the other orders.

Evelyn looks across at Mary Atherton. She is like her husband, slim and silver, elegant. They must have grown like that together. Mary smiles back.

'Are your children still living in Hobart?'

There is a sudden strained silence. She has committed a faux pas. Why had she so readily assumed? But then why not?

Mary's smile tightens briefly, and then relaxes. 'My husband and I have had only one child. Tragically, she died some years ago. So, tell me, do you mind being on your own for all that time in the bush?'

This is a serious question for Evelyn. For reasons not entirely clear to her, and despite what she has defiantly said to Graeme on the matter, she is considerably apprehensive, even at moments fearful, at the prospect of spending such an extended period far away from anywhere and anyone. On the other hand, she genuinely welcomes the opportunity to prove to herself and to the greater world her self-reliance and self-command. A thing like this would not faze her mother, nor does she think it is worrying Joseph overly. For her it is a challenge, which is the very reason she must rise up to it.

'Well, in many ways, I like doing things on my own. I felt very happy on the little trip I've just made, happier than I've felt in a long time. Also, I tend to become jealous of my own areas of research, and I must confess I don't respond well to authority. I always find myself fighting against it, even if I think it's right.'

'Why?' Mary asks.

'I don't know. I guess I'm scared of being overwhelmed, scared I might lose myself in someone or something, lose sense of myself, like happens occasionally in the wilderness for example. Surely you've have felt that power out in the bush.'

'I have felt it, certainly,' replies the professor, 'but I don't think I've ever felt the need to fight it. You do?'

'I do, I don't. It seems to me finally that either someone or something dominates you or you dominate it. What's the alternative?'

'What about the idea of dialogue?' asks Mary.

'A dialogue with the wilderness?' Evelyn replies, examining her. She has a kind, even noble, face, especially her eyes, which are a soft brown. A smattering of surviving freckles adds a girlish touch, strangely not incongruous in such a mature assured figure.

'Sure,' says Joseph, 'Mary is right. That's the way I feel. Look at the moon.'

They all turn back to the window. The bow, silver and cold, hangs poised over the still black bay.

'The moon,' continues Joseph 'has a dialogue with our earth. Both influence one another, to some extent depend on one another, yet it's as necessary that they're separate, as it is that they interact, balanced between gravity and centrifugal force. If that balance, that distance which allows their dialogue, is disturbed to a point of collapse, either the moon crashes into the earth, or it spins off into space. Either way the result is chaos for one or both parties. The earth and the moon have mutual respect. Such a dialogue is possible with the wilderness. In fact, I think it's essential.'

Does he sound like a fool again? Beer always makes him gabble, and then at some point takes away his power of speech entirely. On the other hand, he does believe in what he has said, and he sees that Evelyn has listened closely.

'You make it sound so easy,' she says, still staring out at the night. 'I do try and communicate, constantly, but it seems so difficult. All my efforts seem to be misdirected, misunderstood, and then I think, well, what's the use?'

'But as you said, what's the alternative?' says Joseph.

'But do you really think it can exist, genuine dialogue?' she turns back to him.

He cannot read her look. 'Certainly.'

'And complete understanding?'

'No... Perhaps in special circumstances, but significant understanding, sure.'

'I don't know.'

The wine arrives. Evelyn sips her glass gingerly. She looks out again at the moon. Joseph's little speech sounded rehearsed, like some standard Wilderness Society spiel. She knows he is sincere, but the moon and the earth: it's just too simplistic to apply it to man and nature.

'Tell me, Joseph,' she says leaning in towards him, 'how much of the state is still forested?'

'Forty per cent, more or less.'

'Sounds quite a lot.'

'Think rather of how much has been lost. It's difficult to imagine what this place must have looked like in the early years of the colony, the size of some of the trees, the range of the forests. There are many accounts of axemen taking days to fell swamp gum, mountain ash as you call it on the mainland.'

'But obviously, there's still plenty of all that left.'

'There won't be unless we act. Look what happened to Lake Pedder. It was flooded the same year the export woodchipping started.'

'A portent, you think. Did you ever see the beach at Pedder?'

'I played on it many times as a kid. My father is an amateur pilot. As a young man, he used to work at the Hydro Commission in the same section as the wilderness photographer Olegas Truchanas. He used to fly him in with all his equipment, and often take me along.'

'You knew Olegas Truchanas?'

'As a kid, before he drowned. His protégé, another wonderful wildlife photographer, Peter Dombrowskis, is a close friend. I don't know whether you've heard of him too. They are our modern Glovers and Piguenits, our modern landscape painters. Of course it's all good propaganda too, but also it's great art, great art with a cause. But nothing can match the actual experience. They know that, so that reverence, the awe for what's out there, comes through all their work, just as it does with those painters.'

'When I was at your cousin's hotel in Devonport, I briefly met the mayor, Tony Warne. Do you know him?'

'The credible face of conservatism. No, I shouldn't say that. Tony's a nice guy, I just don't agree with his opinions.'

'Well, I won't even ask you about the plantations. But do you think a native forest can regenerate satisfactorily after clear-felling?'

'The old-growth forests are a kind of living fossil, part of the original Gondwanaland, the first land mass. The various interlocking ecosystems here are incredibly old. You cut down even part of it, and something different will grow back. So, basically, it's irreplaceable, but incredibly the idea is still ingrained in the government and the bureaucracy that this is all simply a resource to be exploited. Nothing has changed in that regard since the Van Diemen's Land days.'

'Except that organisations like yours are springing up.'

'And that's largely because while the head-in-the-sand attitudes here have not changed, the world has. The planet is shrinking, and human population is exploding. We stand in these forests and they seem immense and timeless, but unless we act now their days are numbered. We can still experience them, but perhaps our children will only read about them, look at the beautiful paintings and photographs.'

'You agree with all this, professor?'

'Joseph could be my spokesman.'

Yes, she's in partisan territory here. Not much point in bringing up Tony Warne's question about jobs. It would just start an argument in which she would be out of her depth.

The food arrives. There is a bit of welcome bustle as they reorganise the table and eat in companionable silence. The waiter was right; the curry is hot. She takes her time.

'So, have you got anything planned for tomorrow?' Mary asks Evelyn.

'I thought I'd drive out and see Maria Island. Since it's both an old convict settlement and a wildlife sanctuary, I can kill two birds with one stone.'

'Not a good metaphor for a zoologist,' Mary smiles.

Evelyn laughs and Joseph is amazed how it changes her face. He has not seen her laugh.

'I don't know much about the place,' says Evelyn, 'the wildlife part, I mean.'

'In the late sixties, Maria Island was established as a refuge for threatened species,' replies the professor. 'There was a big sponsorship at the time by the World Wildlife Fund to find a Tasmanian tiger. The original plan was for tigers to be moved there and left to breed in safety. That didn't happen of course, but other animals have been introduced, Forrester kangaroos, for example.'

'Joseph mentioned to me there have been reported tiger sightings from the Walls.'

'Yes,' replied the professor. 'Just the usual unverifiable stuff from campers.'

'I can believe the sightings. There is a large dog or something around Dixon-Kingdom hut. I saw it myself.'

'Right. So it's a dog.'

'Pretty sure. It was dark and I didn't really get a good look.'

'It's probably a beagle,' says Joseph.

'Why a beagle?' asks Evelyn.

'One evening two years ago, out near the Walls, I was convinced I saw a Tasmanian tiger. The sun had just set and there was this doglike creature briefly silhouetted on a high rock. What clinched it in my mind was that, even in that light, the ribcage was clearly visible, just like in the pictures of the tiger, but not like any normal dog.'

'Did you see it again?' asked Evelyn.

'It came into the camp for food. A beagle.'

'What was it doing in the wilderness? How did it get there?'

'My companion, who grew up on a farm, told me that some of the farmers regularly, illegally, venture into the parks to catch game, wallabies mainly. They take hunting dogs with them, trained beagles. They're not too fussed about rounding up the dogs when they've finished their sport.'

'And the ribs?'

'The thing was starving. It was quite tame, we brought it back with us. Interesting how one's mind, and certain effects, can very easily play tricks.'

'Did the tiger used to be common in the area?'

'Yes, and I knew that, and that's partly why I was fooled.' Joseph wonders whether he has dominated too much of the conversation up to this point. It's time to anticipate the beer's eventual effect and fall silent, let others pick up the thread.

The professor obliges. 'Although long extinct, Evelyn, the tiger still has quite a presence down here. It's a little like the Loch Ness monster, a bit of a Tasmanian joke. People see it from time to time even though nobody really thinks it exists. There hasn't been an actual body produced since the 1930s, and no skin or bones since then, just a few suspect photos and footprints.'

'Still,' she replies, 'I suppose it has happened before. Everyone thought the coelacanth was extinct.'

'That's a deep-sea fish. Go down a few fathoms and we don't know much about the ocean at all. This is a big land carnivore we're talking about, requiring a large feeding range and a much larger breeding area. And on a relatively small island, even if much of it still remains unexplored and uninhabitable. But there are plenty of "tiger tragics" out there, even among the scientific community. So, to cover our tracks, so to speak, it might be a good idea to brief you on the tiger before you return to the Walls, show that we're taking these sightings seriously. A colleague of mine at the university, Bob Baines, is a specialist on carnivorous marsupials. He probably knows more about the thylacine than anyone. Are you interested in seeing him?'

'Yes, of course.'

'I'll set it up.'

Maria Island

As Evelyn leans in to examine the tiger, the surrounds become increasingly blurred. There is rough, almost abstract, brushwork beginning at the edges, the raw off-white canvas, gradually becoming hills, bushes, trees, rocks, and a finely rendered creek bed, from which the exquisitely detailed creature (water dripping from its shining snout) looks up towards some unseen adversary beyond the blackwood frame. She continues towards the short-haired flanks taut over bunched muscle and sinew, and it all collapses to brushwork again. There is a point at which she thinks if she closes in she will see more. But when she does, that more dissolves.

'I don't know, Amy. Perhaps it wasn't big enough or something. He was English, you said. Maybe he had that horse painter, Stubbs, in mind, you know, the individual thing, large and plain. He asked for a tiger and you gave him a landscape.'

'I've given him both, my dear. One can't exist without the other.'

True, and Evelyn can't really argue against such excellent work.

'There would be a visual equivalent of "tin ear".'

'It was a fancy of his, a scientist commissioning a picture. He was flattering himself or something. When they couldn't find any tigers after all, and the whole Maria Island thing was mothballed, and he had to go home, he dropped it. That's all.'

'Surely you could have pushed him. A deal's a deal.'

'I didn't really need the money, and if he didn't want it, for whatever reason, after all my effort, I didn't want him to have it. Customer satisfaction is half the point, and anyway, I've enjoyed it down the years. I did some sketches for it *en plein air*. I'll show you where on your tourist map if you're interested.'

'Sure, yes, I'll seek out the place.'

They are in Amy's studio, a converted colonial warehouse on the waterfront, big rough wood beams, high ceiling, clear shaded light. Amy has risen well before Evelyn. She is an habitual early riser, so Evelyn has dropped in for a cuppa en route to Maria Island. Amy is showing her some of her work; all landscapes, at least what is here, mostly in gouache with an intentional eighteenth century 'pictorial' effect. Claude an obvious influence, and the local, John Glover.

'Do you sell much?'

'Not at the moment. Since I only tend to do the one type of thing, it goes in and out of fashion. Plus Hobart is a modest market and I've pretty much exhausted it.'

'What about the big cities?'

'That's where you get the fashion. Had a good show in Melbourne two years back. Fortunately, the stuff's decorative, so if they're willing to push it, it will move.'

'One day I'll come back and buy one.'

Evelyn isn't just making talk, she is genuinely taken, and taken aback too by Amy's commitment. An eccentric great-aunt perhaps, but she is also, Evelyn sees, a considerable talent, a force as well in her own way, determined and focused. In that way like her mother, and like she herself wishes to be. Coming out of the generation she did, Amy made a decision not to marry and have children because she wanted to paint, seriously. And she has, and Evelyn admires her for it.

'I suppose I'd better get moving.'

'Still early, and you've got the day for it.'

Hot and still, summer's last throw. The heat is delightful to Evelyn because it is dry, not the endless sauna of a Sydney summer. A hot day in a cool climate. She leaves Amy to her work, driving north across flat peninsulas and around sparkling bays. She has to reach the small holiday resort of Triabunna, two hours away, before the single ferry for the day leaves at 10.30.

She arrives in ample time, needlessly, as the boat is running forty-five minutes late. At 10.30 she is sitting on the jetty with a handful of tourists and locals watching it gradually approach from a distance. This increasingly irritates her. Conditions are perfect, so why is the boat late? She has to keep telling herself everything is fine. It is pleasant sitting in the sun looking out across the bay at the blue distance. She is not a good sea traveller and could not have asked for calmer weather. She is in no hurry to go anywhere; she is sightseeing, should be enjoying herself, unreservedly, but still, the boat should not be late.

Finally, with a great clang of reversing engines, it lists into the dock. Long lee waves slap up, spraying people and luggage, and if that is not enough, the captain gratuitously sounds a great horn blast scattering gulls and pigeons into the bright air. He appears scowling on the bridge, a compact apoplectic Napoleon, and with no word of explanation, strides down the steps, across the gangplank, and disappears into one of the shops, leaving his craft rocking gently at the jetty.

They all clamber aboard and Evelyn sits tight with the others, impatiently waiting his return. Opposite her is a puffy anxious man in his mid-thirties with a pasty face, prominent jowls and thick closely cropped grey hair. He wears a tatty green jumper with the sleeves rolled up and no shirt underneath. He continuously pulls a cigarette in and out of his mouth and fiddles with it. She closes her eyes against him and listens to the soothing slow slap of the waves against the hull.

'Moind if we sit 'ere?' The ugliness of the high-pitched accent is like fingernails on a blackboard.

'No, of course not.'

She opens her eyes to the woman and her children. In her twenties but unnaturally thin, a dried brown face and lank straggly black hair, wearing a simple Indian-style grubby white cotton shift. Motherhood, it seems, does not agree with her. Her children in contrast are blooming: a cherub infant she proceeds to feed with a bottle, and two girls who are arguing over possession of a doll. It is evident they have been arguing all morning.

The woman turns suddenly and screams at them, 'Shut up, you two, or I'll take you 'ome!'

The girls pause for a breather, then resume their quarrel.

Evelyn shifts to the other side of the boat. Better to stand for the length of the journey than put up with that. She thinks, this woman briefly hates her children even while she loves them. And that baby with a bottle: the human spawn is so helpless and dependent; so much we must be taught to cope with the world and its demands, more than any other creature.

She stares over into the still cold water in the shadow of the hull, watching the shifting rainbows of immiscible surface oil. She lets her mind drift with the colours, loses sense of time. Finally, the captain returns, and with much fussing and shouting the engine sputters to life and they cast off.

Evelyn leans on the varnished stern rail, vibrating warmly, and watches sea and coast slip away. The light is glorious, beyond the ferry's spreading wake the water hasn't a ripple. Either it is gleamless or, more accurately, it reflects one light, is one immense illuminated surface. The rich green coast moves past her and away with an exaggerated slowness; the movement can just be perceived if mind and eye are sufficiently attuned. The minute hand of a clock. A plant opening to the sun. And in the distance the double bulk of Maria Island grows with the same barely perceptible compulsion.

Occasionally she is jerked back to attention by a sudden close movement or noise, but the calm reasserts itself, more powerfully and for longer periods, so she is surprised to find the boat gliding into dock at the scrub-covered land.

For the first time, although she has been staring at it for almost two hours, Evelyn notices the colour of the water, a transparent aqua. She can see straight to the sandy bottom, observe schools of fish and clumps of seagrass. It looks tropical, but she knows it is cold. She also knows that the whole alluring eastern coastline of Tasmania is deceptively treacherous. Beneath these clean bright waters lurk shoals and shallows and sandbanks that are a mariner's nightmare and have proved the graveyard of countless vessels.

More stentorian shouting. They alight, and Evelyn shuffles behind the others down a rickety jetty towards a colonial stone storage building refurbished as an information centre. She glances at the brochures, the story of the convicts, their grim privations and the grisly details of their sufferings. She really just wants to wander around the island in the sun and see the surviving marks of brutality and cruelty as an ignorant tourist might, as picturesque ruins. Also, to find the gully and creek in Amy's painting.

She walks back out into the bright light. Now the sun is at its height. The other tourists are filing along a dirt road leading on through tall casuarinas to the old penal settlement. She sets off the opposite way, up a dry grassy hill. Large swaths of gold beat in slow uneven waves in the warm wind, but there seems to be no wind at all on the sea, shining at a distance like the surface of an opal. In and about the grass bob brown heads of Bennett's wallabies. They casually hop away if she approaches. As she labours upwards, the waving grass, the sea and the light again seem to cast a spell. She is walking through an idyll of Streeton's, a timeless, golden land of sun and sea.

On the crest is a small separate prison, a square cottage constructed of large irregular convict-cut blocks. In the shadow of one of the walls lies a sick wallaby, every few moments compulsively raking its left foot in the dust. Its companions avoid it, in silently cruel but completely natural recognition that sickness does not belong to life. When Evelyn approaches, the animal attempts to rise and then subsides. She bends close and examines it. No obvious injuries. It is panting heavily but this might simply be stress from her presence. The door of the prison has a modern Do Not Enter sign nailed on. She tries the heavy lock and it opens easily.

Inside, the floor has rotted away and there is a sharp stagnant smell. It is surprisingly cold. The building consists of two small rooms connected by a low stone doorway from which a door has also decayed.

There is a tiny window in each room to let in a minimum of light, too high to allow inmates the luxury of a view. Evelyn imagines that on a day like today a prisoner with any chance of escape would contemplate the long swim to the mainland with some hope. Certainly, the beauty of the surrounds provides stark contrast to the prospect of incarceration in a hole like this.

She steps over into the second room. Nothing. Why have they closed the building? Is it dangerous? There appears to be some graffiti in one bottom corner. Just odd marks on the stone, although they do look as if they have been carved. One of the rock pieces above is oddly shaped and slightly protuberant. Evelyn dislodges it easily. Then on a hunch, she reaches in behind the wall, where she grasps the metal hilt of, bringing it out, a large rusty knife, rough and handmade. The blade is long and curved like a small scimitar. So, to what savage did this belong, and for what purpose? Protection? Murder? She shivers. The dark of the stone prison and the chill air has caught the sweat on her back from the climb. She slips the knife into her canvas satchel with her jumper and purse.

Back outside, she wanders further up to some cliffs, which have been quarried (the endless daily grind), then looks for the place where Amy has marked her map. She finds it, seemingly little changed in the intervening years. Descending to the creek bed, Evelyn tries to locate the precise spot where Amy's imaginary tiger was crouching and when she thinks she is there, on a whim, she poses like the animal, bending down and looking up over her shoulder. What did it see or hear? A wallaby or a man? Something it might hunt, or something that might hunt it? Her satchel rides high on her back as she bends awkwardly. The convict knife tumbles out over her shoulder and clatters on the rocks, startling her. She retrieves the knife, and makes her way across to the penal station, which by now most of the others have left.

There is a macabre museum with instruments of punishment, notably cat o' nines and the notorious triangles. While outside, the sun is shining and birds are singing. It all seems so absurd, so unnecessary.

Is it largely a male thing? Men together without women, or without admitting women's influence, always seem to produce a brutal stratified society, and no doubt to the misery of most of the men within it.

Three loud horn blasts. Napoleon and his ferry.

'Lumpy jaw: this is what we're most interested in with you, of course, but this is an opportunity for us to get really good feedback on the Walls. You've plenty of time. Anything at all that strikes you as interesting, feel welcome to pursue.'

'Like that dog, for instance?'

'Keep me in touch on the dog – we may have to send in a team. But more generally, feel free to, I don't know, range.'

Range. Facing the professor now, she feels very strongly that, as the junior member of the team, she must do as well as the others, if not better. Prove her place. Here is her own little nascent struggle for existence, before she hits professional academia, genuinely red in tooth and claw.

'There was nothing damaged in the first drop?'

'Everything seemed fine.'

'I'll be organising two more drops per park. Food, bait and traps. I need you to tell me exactly what you want and when you want it, and I'll make sure it happens.'

'I may as well take a couple of traps in the car, in addition to the tracking equipment. Make some trips in and out.'

'And you'll be taking in the radio.'

'I've already put up the aerial.'

'Good. I expect you to contact me every forty-eight hours. If you miss two contacts, I'll initiate standard search and rescue procedures.'

They are in the professor's roomy office, which unlike him, surprisingly, is a mess. His alter ego presumably, private wilderness. There are books and magazines piled up randomly, specimen cases, cork-stoppered jars containing what appear to be mammal foetuses, although Evelyn doesn't look too closely, and a large doglike skull commanding a cluttered desk.

'Professor, can you give me a little more leeway with the contact stuff?'

'Why?'

'Couple of reasons. The Walls are very isolated and radio transmission is going to be difficult at times. Plus I'll be working irregular hours. I'd really hate it if I missed a couple of contacts and search and rescue came in and nothing was wrong. I can see it happening. Can you make the official time frame every four days but I promise to ring you more than that?'

'All right, Evelyn, as long as I have regular contacts.'

'Of course.' She looks at the skull. 'That's not a thylacine?'

'Alaskan timber wolf, from my first paying job.'

After her briefing, they descend for lunch to the student cafeteria. A cheap seventies addition to the campus, bright moulded plastic, deep-fried everything, dishwater coffee. Evelyn settles for a tea bag. She knows she can't go too wrong and she's getting tired of Amy's herbals, but the professor loads right up on his carbohydrates, and even has a couple of beers to wash it all down. Good candidate for lumpy jaw.

'You sure you're not hungry?'

'I'll get a sandwich later.'

'How did you enjoy Maria Island?'

'Didn't really take it all in – the convict stuff, I mean. A bit heavy for a summer's day outing.'

'You mainlanders come down to drive through a picture postcard, either not thinking or not knowing that Van Diemen's Land was the most brutal penal colony of its kind, and how much our early history is soaked in blood. White blood, black blood.'

'That's the same for much of the country.'

'But here particularly. One finds a sign occasionally, ploughs up an instrument of oppression, or a weapon, or hears odd tales still surviving in remote communities of general savagery, indigenous massacres and even cannibalism among the escaped convicts.'

The professor seems to be shifting into pedagogue mode – he is a professional lecturer – or maybe it's the beers. Evelyn doesn't mind; she is tired of talking zoology, and always happy to learn. She feels very comfortable with the professor. Perhaps because she has never really had this avuncular – no, let's be honest here, fatherly – mature relationship with a man. She settles back and sips her tea.

'Wasn't the Walls a popular hiding spot for convicts?'

'…turned cannibals and bushrangers. They all had a price on their heads. If you had guts and you wanted to make a bit of money, you could take your gun into the Central Ranges and try your luck. The government required you to bring back the head of your quarry for proof of payment. Michael Howe, one of the most notorious bushrangers, operated in the Walls. He was shot in a stock hut in 1818 and his head was brought back to Hobart Town hanging from a saddle to great acclaim.'

'How horrible,' says Evelyn, thrilled. 'In a way, cannibalism is the ultimate human degradation.'

'Not compared to what they suffered before they escaped, as you saw. The military officers and the government had virtually unlimited power, and they weren't any less brutal than the men they managed. They kept the women for sex and flogged the men to impossible labour and death.'

'Cannibals in the Central Ranges. And here I am a hundred and fifty years later studying the effects of degradation on the environment by hikers. How weird.'

'Well, Evelyn, your work is important, I didn't mean to belittle it by comparison. Of course, Hobart is civilised and peaceful, but all this was not so long ago. My ancestors, as a matter of fact. Joseph's too. Civilisation is a fragile contract, a fragile dialogue, to use Mary's term from the other night.'

'It's an interesting idea. Among all the other things, out in the bush I'm trying to construct a dialogue.'

'Or understand an existing one.'

'Yes. I'll have to see how that works out.'

Professor Atherton takes Evelyn to Bob Baines's house as promised. When they arrive, he is practising the piano, and his wife brusquely asks the visitors to wait.

'Only another fifteen minutes. Robert always plays for an hour exactly. He has a strict routine. It's important his concentration isn't broken.'

Funny approach to music, thinks Evelyn. Mrs Baines possesses a fluty cultured voice. She is tall and grand and, even though it's just a normal weekday afternoon, clad in a long glittering blue dress of a type Amy Meadows might well buy in an op shop fifteen years down the track and wear with a coat and sandshoes. The three of them sit in silence and listen to the crash and run of keys from the adjoining room.

Professor Baines can undoubtedly play. Indeed, Professor Atherton settles into the performance, but the flashy skill piques Evelyn. She is aware of being jealous of the man's talent even though she has no desire to gain it.

She dwells on this. The sensation is similar to one she has begun to feel towards Amy and the Athertons. She tries to locate it. She envies them their happiness, their contentment: that is it, she thinks. This is a recurrent problem of hers, causing all kinds of dislocations in living arrangements during her student days. If she is thrown close to people, it seems that only their suffering ever really engages her sympathies. Another reason she is better on her own.

But of all interpersonal antipathies, there is nothing that sets her teeth more on edge than seeing what she considers her own faults reflected in others. In contrast to his wife, Professor Baines is nervous, lacking in personal self-confidence. He even smells a little, falls over himself with apologies when he realises he has kept guests waiting, and keeps referring back to it guiltily. Evelyn feels a headache immediately, and resists a sudden strong irrational urge to scream and exit the room.

She clamps down on herself and, after the usual formalities, calmly encourages Bob Baines, a 'tiger tragic' if ever there were one, to communicate his considerable and fascinating knowledge.

'If by some extraordinary chance, this is a thylacine, then, as you are a trained zoologist, you are in a very fortunate position to follow up. You will be alone in the park for a number of months, and there will be no one else around to disturb the animal if the hut is in its territory. They are territorial beasts, you know. But anyway, we need to know whether, far more likely, it's a dog or a feral cat.'

He avoids looking at her while addressing her. She is grateful for that.

'It definitely wasn't a cat.'

'Did you see it clearly, Miss Carter? Was there any moonlight?'

'No, there was no moon...' she remembers the stars '...but it was much too big for a cat. I'm sure about that.'

'You might be surprised. Feral cats are the biggest wildlife problem in Australia, no doubt, you know. I've seen some pretty large pussies running around in the bush. Some have even attacked farmer's dogs. So, do you know much about the thylacine?'

'Not really.'

'Here's an old photograph of the last surviving male in the Hobart Beaumaris Zoo from the 1930s. Please look at it carefully. You see the animal is most similar to a wolf or dog in appearance. It has a large head, evenly balanced backbone, deep chest, non-retractable claws, runs on its toes and not on its heels but, of course, it is a marsupial.'

Evelyn examines the grainy black-and-white print intently. It seems strangely tragic, life caught, life no longer. An image that tells us much about an extinct animal, and by extension something also about ourselves. She tries to recall those few moments in the dark, but can only clearly recall her fear.

'What size does it grow to?'

'A little over two metres in length. Longevity about thirteen to fourteen years, again like a dog.'

'Much difference between male and female?'

'The female is more like a bulldog with a short skull, and the male more like a greyhound. It has a sandy-coloured body, higher on the stomach, short thick hair…the most obvious features, of course, are the stripes or bands on the back and the rump, about thirteen to nineteen, dark brown coloured, consistent with animals camouflaged by adaptation to woodland conditions. The bands are more prominent in younger animals. The female's pouch faces backwards, the tail is long and stiff, the creature by all accounts is reasonably docile towards man…'

'Have there been recent sightings other than the Walls?'

'There are always sightings from Woolnorth, the Van Diemen's Land Company up in the far north-west, and I personally believe there are still a few tigers up there. But it's private property, and they won't let us on. Don't blame them. If a tiger was positively sighted or caught at Woolnorth, there would be immense pressure on the company to forgo its land. If there are tigers up there, they are quite safe for the present. Private property's probably the best place for them.'

This runs counter to a few of Evelyn's beliefs. She digests the information.

'It's funny,' she says, 'with the bounty on their pelts that they weren't hunted to extinction on private property, if they were elsewhere.'

'Well, they weren't really hunted to extinction, you see. It was more a bad combination of events. The tigers were never very frequent even in colonial times. The farmers lost far more sheep from stealing and stray dogs than from thylacines. Anyway, late last century they seemed to undergo a population rise, and as you mentioned, the government put a bounty on their skins. Each year many were shot, but then in 1909–1910 they seemed to suddenly disappear without a trace, virtually the entire population. Can't be attributed to the bounty.'

'Then?'

'Some form of distemper-like disease at the time felled all carnivorous marsupials. Even the devils only really recovered their numbers in the 1940s. The bounty didn't help. The government dropped it in the 1930s but it was too late. Hardly any thylacines were shot after 1910. There have been good persistent reports of sightings, tracks, etcetera up until the late fifties, but no one has actually shot or photographed one, so the status of the species must remain in doubt. We even get occasional reports from the mainland, particularly the Nullarbor, although I'm disinclined to believe these, as Aborigines report no sightings and fossil records show no thylacines have lived on mainland Australia for thousands of years. The dingo was simply a much more efficient predator. Anyway, as you know, much of Tasmania is still wild. If thylacines do still exist, there is every reason to believe they can build back their population. It remains to be seen, I suppose.'

'You haven't seen one, Professor Baines?'

'Unfortunately, no.' He stops for a moment as though he has lost his voice. 'Is there anything else you want to know?'

Professor Atherton looks up at Evelyn, who is both fascinated with what has been said, and dying to get away. Her headache is now definitely at problem level.

'No,' she says, 'Thank you very much for your time. I'm afraid I'm not well and really need to get home and lie down.'

Storm

The sky from Hobart to Devonport is thinly overcast, but once back on the road approaching the plateau, it closes in. Typically, no actual rain falls until Evelyn parks and gets out. On the other hand, she considers, if it had come down any earlier, she might not have made it this far.

From all the stuff thrown haphazardly into the boot and back seat, her own gear and what the professor has provided, she carefully places in her pack, on top of the tent and sleeping bag, those items essential for setting up the hut. Or if she doesn't make the hut, what she will strictly need for holing out a few days in the tent. She methodically dons standard wet-weather gear: gloves, parka, plastic pants, and clips snow gaiters in the crossed laces down the front of her boots, strapping them firmly behind her calves. The wind is cold and strong and might carry snow or sleet by the time she reaches the plateau. Maybe it is snowing there now, although the clouds still look like rain clouds, lacking that strange dirty mustard that signals snow. She locks up, hoists her load, and sets off.

Ten minutes and she is warming up and feeling more positive. It is a long trek and will be uncomfortable walking through rain and slush, and also boring, but if the weather stays much as it is, there should be no great trouble in reaching the hut in four or five hours. She has plenty of daylight.

The wet flushes out the strong smells of the bush: gums, moss, bark, earth. The forest seems to inhale, come to life, with the rain. As will the leeches, no doubt. Not to worry; she will deal with them later. She finds the climbing easier than before. She is fitter, but the real difference is the drop in temperature, no more enervating heat. As she rises, the wind steadily increases, smarting cold against her cheeks, she can feel them glowing, but still not cold enough for snow.

Once up on the plateau, with wind and rain settling into a rhythm, the front established, Evelyn sees from here on it will be one hard slog. She pushes on without a break. The track turns boggy, remains walkable, but will not be in a couple of hours – she has seen this terrain quickly dissolve into swamp. But then in a couple of hours she will be higher, and hopefully the ground firmer and drier. The open bush is scraggly and dull grey in the wet. She moves quickly as she can, while she can, stomping through the sticky mud. Despite the rain, she is still warm and has plenty of strength.

An hour and a half later, she is at Solomon's Jewels, and the weather has deteriorated. She appears to be walking into a storm. A break for a drink and some chocolate. She can't decide if it would be better to stop here, set up a tent and bunker in. She can now dimly see the mass of the Walls and Herod's Gate, but only through odd breaks in the wide sheets of rain. Beyond the small forest past the Jewels is the open plain leading to the Gate; this and the saddle before the pine forest after she passes through the main area of the Walls are the most exposed parts of the walk. She can give it a try and if things get too tough, make her way back to the Jewels with the wind behind her. If she reaches the Walls, she can probably find a camping spot near the shelter of one of the cliffs.

She continues through the trees, then emerges onto the wide valley or saddle leading down to Wild Dog Creek and up to Herod's Gate. At once she feels the effect of the more open country. She steadies herself against the wind, looks over to her right but cannot see the Cradle Mountain range. She cannot see the edge of the plateau either and it is only a kilometre away, because that is also where the storm is sweeping in from, as usual, the wild south-western ranges.

Despite her restricted view, there is a sense of immensity in the surrounds; an effect conveyed chiefly by the shifting formations of the storm. From across towards the plateau edge, a continual sequence of enormous whole sheets or blocks of shattered water are marching towards her at a frightening speed. It makes her giddy to watch them. The light is still good, so that her vision extends further vertically than horizontally and that, with the visible hugeness of the weather, makes Evelyn feel she has happened into a world of dimensions different to any she has known, a world to which she, human and inconsequential, does not belong.

But she can still see all this. It is a risk walking out into it, but a calculable one. The ground here is solid and the track plain. If the weather gets no worse in the next hour, she should make the relative shelter of the Walls. While the track remains visible, she cannot get lost. The lie of the land is plain as well, down to the creek, up to the Walls. The track cuts the saddle dead centre, forming a cross with the creek. If she loses the track and the land starts to fall steeply and she does not strike the creek, she knows to turn back. After the creek she only has to make sure she keeps walking up. Once at the Walls, it is only another hour to the hut. She screws up her courage and pushes on.

Now the going gets seriously tough and Evelyn wonders if she is being foolish. Hubris is a not uncommonly fatal flaw for fit hard walkers. Wind and rain lash her ceaselessly, stinging her eyes and making her nose run. It feels freezing, but it is not yet sleet or snow, and it is not stopping her, although it must be slowing her. She looks at her watch; she is a bit behind but there are still plenty of hours. It is important at this juncture that she make a conscious effort to maintain pace, not only because of time but also for body heat. If she has to stop for any reason, she will need to find a place to pitch the tent, and although that seems impossible on this open land, she knows it can be done.

Crouched over with her pack, Evelyn follows the rocky trail doggedly, carefully placing her boots, mindful of twisted ankles. Her spirits begin to waver and her mind to be imaginatively peopled by lost souls who have perished in the area, even on this very stretch. Most were ill-equipped or inexperienced, but some were simply unlucky, had accidentally damaged or lost part of their gear, or suffered sudden injury. This last is a thing no walker can completely guard against. If she were to do her ankle or knee badly on these wet rocky paths, she could be finished. So easy with the pack bearing down, ready to unbalance her and exacerbate any fall.

She has friends who have pitched tents in worse conditions. As night approaches, she knows the tent will stiffen, and so will she. It will be difficult and painful to tie nylon ropes with frozen hands. If she cannot manage it, as a last resort she can wrap herself in the tent. The important thing, always, is to keep dry. The rain is working to make her wet and cold as itself and the earth, one with these smoking plains.

She mentally rehearses the symptoms of hypothermia, the rapid physical and mental collapse that accompanies the chilling of the body's inner core: persistent shivering, then, in short succession, brief euphoria, loss of muscular power, staggering, mental and physical lethargy, vague and slurred speech, frequent stumbling and irrational behaviour. In advanced cases, the shivering stops; bizarrely sometimes the victim experiences a hot flush as contracted muscles fail and blood flows back to the skin. These are the real danger signs, the brain losing control. Unconsciousness and death quickly follow.

She does not feel any of these symptoms now, has never felt them, but has observed them. Once, walking in the Snowy Mountains on the Victorian border in midsummer, it had unseasonably snowed, and one of her party, unfit and lightly clad, started to dance and laugh in a slightly hysterical fashion. Everyone took it for a joke, but then his speech became incoherent and they immediately set up a tent and bundled him into a sleeping bag with one of the party. He had recovered readily, but the incident had occurred so quickly it had shocked her. The body is a remarkable citadel, and she is used to taking her strong constitution for granted, but she knows anyone is vulnerable. In critical conditions, if things go wrong they generally go wrong quickly. The logbooks in the huts in the area are full of grim tales, and there is a wealth of local folklore about privations endured by trappers in times past.

One of these from her reading comes vividly to mind, of a snarer, Bill Nutting, who used to work the country between the Ironstones and the Walls. In 1927, he went up with two horses. Later, the horses came out of the area alone and in bad condition. It was a winter of severe snow, and efforts to find the man failed. The following year, when cattle were driven up to the Walls, the leading cattle gathered in the vicinity of Long Tarns, and Nutting's preserved body was found surrounded by dead matches.

The track suddenly lurches down steeply and she is at Wild Dog Creek, now a boiling brook pocked with rain. She wades through the brown flow and toils up the final stretch towards the Walls. Here the path is badly eroded and has become a little creek itself. She places her feet carefully on the slippery rocks. The weather has not worsened since Solomon's Jewels, maybe the storm is at its height. Now she will make the Walls, if not the hut.

But she is feeling miserable, her clothes are damp and heavy, and water is sloshing in her boots. She is not yet cold but drawing on considerable reserves of willpower to keep moving. Despite all her determination, her body is showing the strain. Intermittent sharp pains in her ankles and knees send out unmistakable signs; her back is aching from being forced over with the pack. Increasingly, she places her feet inaccurately, slipping and stumbling, frightening herself and wasting vital energy. She scrambles up the last of the braided stream that has been the path and through Herod's Gate, not pausing to look back at the wild expanse just traversed.

The huge Western Wall offers some respite and she hugs it closely, wary of rockfalls. There are relatively safe camping spots here, but she might as well push on to the climb up to the saddle of Damascus Gate while she can. The ground is secure; it is simply a matter of keeping on.

Another forty minutes and she is at the foot of the steep rise leading up to the Gate. This is the last pinch, the toughest thing she must do. Once at the top, it is only twenty minutes downhill through the pencil pine forest to the hut. She screws up her will to a pitch.

Shelter and a fire. Again, the path is a stream. As she gropes for hand and footholds on the smooth loose rocks, the freezing water flows down over her arms and legs, seeps beneath her clothing. She is weary and now also a little chilled. Coldness means fatigue. But she is almost there; just keep it up, hand over foot. The flow of water abates as she approaches the top and the path levels out. She rises up on to the saddle and meets the full force of the storm again. Then a fierce individual burst, like a huge fist, catches her unawares and knocks her to her knees. She scrambles up immediately and, hunched double against the wind and sleet and rain, tacks steadily towards the forest two hundred metres away. Huge swaths of icy mist and water slap into her, hail stings her face. Willing one step after another, she finally reaches the shelter of the trees.

She pauses on a rock behind a broad pine trunk to gather her wits and strength. She shouldn't stop for long, but the worst is over. Soon she will be under shelter with a fire crackling out dry heat. The image alone seems to warm her.

Absorbed in her elemental struggles, Evelyn has not considered to what extent the various landscapes she has crossed have been transformed under conditions so radically different to those of her initial trip. Here now, this strikes her, particularly since the change in the pine forest is so marked. Before, the quirky twisted trees seemed a consort of friendly caricatures; she was amused and comforted. Now the forest is spooky, more, distinctly sinister. She blanches at the difference.

Or is it the indifference? For a peculiar thought occurs to her: *à la* Joseph, wilderness might be seen as paradise, but what if paradise is ultimately inhuman? These trees, they exist without her, have no reliance whatever upon her; they existed before her, before all humans; they are not companions, even to environmentalists; they are simply themselves, utterly alien. She shivers, and suddenly, fearfully, feels alone, vulnerable. She must get on, stop thinking, worrying like this.

Tiredness is making her oversensitive. The mist chills, penetrates her clothes. It is thick, a bodily presence; the forest cold and dank. She has walked from a world of vigour, a dangerous tumultuous world of bright hard wind and rain, of open passes and plains, but a world in which she felt she had clear personal definition through her struggle against it. Now here is a world of half-night, half-day, half-storm, half-calm, indefinable, ungraspable, a world she thought she knew but finds she doesn't. The wind has dropped considerably although she can hear it, more clearly it seems now that she's no longer battling it. That weird hollow sound she heard the first night in the hut. Of course, in real terms, in this forest she is substantially less physically threatened than out in the open, so why does she feel unease? She is being irrational.

For here is a palpable calm, but unlike that for which she yearns. The mist blocks her vision in varying and changing degrees, so that large gnarled trees rush out at her, twisted black and dripping. Delightfully grotesque is now ugly and menacing. How can she find a way through? She will become lost, when she is so close, but so tired. She knows the forest is not extensive, and that she needs to simply maintain contour and she will emerge at the hut.

She picks her way through the wet stillness, feeling the level of the ground closely. The air is supersaturated; it's as if she is breathing water. A slick film of moisture coats all hard surfaces, the bark, the rocks; fine droplets embellish the leaves and delicate lichens, while beneath, her boots squelch rotten leaves and layers of soft moss.

She knows she's on the right path when she happens on the same small clearing where she found the dead pademelon. Evelyn recognises the place immediately, completely; for some reason she must have held all the details in the back of her mind. There are no remains left; devils have polished them off. Their scats are around with the larger ones. She has a cursory look. The ground is stained in old blood. Some sort of killing ground for the dog. Must drag its prey here.

Then, standing there in the dead grey light, she is struck by something. The place is pulling at her in some peculiar way, giving to her a sense of déjà vu, or even prevision, seeming to possess, gather into itself, a kind of intensity she can't define.

Perhaps, because the animal has singled out, chosen, no doubt initially out of convenience, this unusually bare patch in a dense forest for a sort of ritual slaughtering, her imagination has been sympathetically stimulated to lend the ground a strange, ceremonial quality. Not dissimilar to what one feels walking out onto an empty theatre stage, or standing at an historic site where some momentous event has occurred. A place where things happen, or might happen. Animal and man. What the beast is unconsciously making here, establishing for itself, is only one step removed from magic, which is only one step removed from religion. Everything traceable back to the wild.

If she finds it, should she kill it? She has never killed anything like that in her life, a big warm-blooded mammal. Or maybe it will be dangerous if it realises it is being threatened. Maybe it is dangerous anyway. She has no gun or poison, she's never even handled a gun. She could cut its throat. That, no doubt, is far more difficult than it sounds. She has a good sharp knife, probably too small, but she has also brought that curio from Maria Island which theoretically could do the job. But kill a large dog single-handedly? No, it's completely beyond her. If she gets another clear sighting, she'll inform the professor and leave it to him and his colleagues.

Continuing through the trees, her spirits revive with the knowledge she must be nearing the hut. The wind picks up. Suddenly she leaves the thick forest growth for the open valley running down to Lake Ball and the storm hits her again, huge silver sheets of it. It has been waiting for her. She panics for a moment, she cannot face another battle, but turns around and sees the hut about a hundred metres up the valley. A final struggle through the long slippery grass, the last short stretch, and she pushes inside and dumps her wet pack on the flagstones.

She staggers around for a few moments, dazed, digesting her relief, although by any ordinary standards the hut is hardly inviting. Old wet cold. There is water dripping from the roof, and a pungent smell of quolls and possums which have sought shelter and food scraps in the absence of campers. No big deal; in time she can patch the leaks. The toilet seems fine and the place is basically clean. First thing needed is a fire. Warmth and light. There is still some dry wood in the fireplace, and also plenty of damp wood stacked in the little sheltered alcove outside the door.

Overcoming a sudden strong lassitude, Evelyn forces herself into organisation and soon a spitting warmth is pushing damp ghosts from the room and her mind. The logs crackle and blaze, returning the light and heat collected once from the sun. She boils a billy and sits close, sipping coffee, eating chocolate, resting, thawing, drying and casting the salted curled bodies of leeches to their purgatory. The storm rages outside. How good she feels. The weather is sounding worse by the minute. She has been lucky to make the hut, and will probably be stuck inside for a couple of days. Better than out there. She has her sleeping bag, sufficient food, and even books and candles. She can wait out the storm comfortably before having to return to the car.

Professor Atherton would probably be aware of the front. She should try and contact him and let him know all is well. She digs the two-way radio from her pack where she has wrapped it carefully in plastic, sets it up and tries his number. Static, but the set seems to be working. The weather is simply too fierce. She'll try again when it eases.

Now somewhat revitalised, Evelyn begins to set out the hut as a home, for this is what it will be for the next few months. She neatly stacks the provisions she has brought on the wooden shelves above the metal cabinet and also makes a separate space on them for her clothes which, despite the rain, are more or less dry. In advance, she works out exactly where she will place all the stuff in the car she still needs to carry in.

The prospect and activity cheer her. She loves putting things in order, placing each object exactly where it should be, and with no one around to interfere. More than that, she enjoys the self-discipline of routine, telling herself what to do and obeying her own dictates, having power over herself, as Graeme often joked. Bustling about, she considers how planning a life, even a short life, in the wilderness is a good exercise for an urbanite. Becoming aware of the essentials of existence, and the superfluities, necessarily throws you back on your own resources.

She's allowed herself a few luxuries: a loaf of bread, some fresh vegetables and a little meat, her coffee percolator, but largely brought in tinned and powdered food, dried vegetables, spices, plenty of rice, equipment and notebooks. Here she is starting life from scratch for a while.

She positions a saucepan under the largest drip. The weather is wild now; furious erratic waves of wind and rain sweep over the hut. The journey in was tough, but there is no way she could have walked through this. She imagines curled up against it in a tent, hour after hour, vainly trying to sleep, dreading having to go out to the toilet, worrying whether the guy lines are secure, chewing scroggin for meals washed down with brackish water.

Evelyn nudges the door open an inch. Nothing but snow mixed with driving rain. A few flakes drift in with the wind. Probably there will be a white-out, but this early in the season she knows the blizzard will blow over and settle into rain. If it is simply raining, she can walk back and get more stuff without much trouble. So for a while nothing matters; she has time, a luxury she can hardly remember, especially craved towards the end of last year with her exams and essay.

More than a luxury, an opportunity. She cannot go out into the field; she is to be left entirely to her own thoughts. Good. When she wishes to, Evelyn can withdraw into herself completely, a character trait, ability, she knows has helped her become a top student. If need be, she can focus at will to block out all extraneous distractions, but here all distractions are removed by circumstance; the storm intensifies her isolation. As she sits hypnotically staring at the dancing flames, she confirms how much she needs this.

Perhaps now she can work through to some considered conclusion the whole painful seemingly inescapable business with men and herself, particularly the latest with Graeme. She must resolve it all.

Since she stepped on the plane, she has sensed it quietly festering away beneath her surface thoughts. Now with the aid of these four blank walls, she will revisit and re-examine the relevant events, hold them up to the harsh light of truth, review injustices, allocate blame, and see how she might anticipate and avoid pain in the future.

She broods darkly into the flames, watching them gradually subside to a film above the logs, which fracture into even grey-red cubes through which tiny electric worms wriggle. Finally, she reaches forward with an old bent poker and smashes the structures down to fitfully glowing white ash amid arabesques of smoke.

Evelyn is not pleased that she has managed a good number of lovers for her age. She has always attracted men easily, but has never desired to move restlessly from one to another as she has found herself doing. This has simply been dislocating. But with every relationship, she seems locked into an inexorable cycle of love, passion, domination, and then loss of libido and interest. And so on to the next.

Graeme fought her the hardest, proving her most damaging and significant relationship to date; for a time she felt, she desperately hoped, it might actually endure, but then the cycle reasserted itself. Finally, it was the same – she no longer wanted him, she wanted one of his closest friends, Brett. In the fraught latter stages of their lovemaking, she had to summon up Brett's image, think it was him touching, needing her. But then it has always been a mystery to her why she physically desires men at all.

Once, she spent an idle hour leafing through some girly magazines left amongst rubbish in a room she had rented, and was amazed to find herself aroused to masturbation. But then it seems she has always preferred women's bodies to men's. The first time she saw a live naked man, she was repelled; her initial sexual fantasies and infatuations at Frensham involved the women around her, and she has often imagined making love to another woman, a thing that has never happened because invariably, disconcertingly, repeatedly she finds herself falling for men. And it is a fact that they can arouse her physically, despite their roughness, lack of understanding and sympathy.

Men have driven her to such extremes against her will, often excited her against her will, made her desire certain things and even initiate acts she has later been ashamed of, behaviour that is not her. She is no radical, but it is not too difficult to see why some women eventually come to reject men, with their self-absorption and bestiality (always there below the surface), and particularly their absolutely incredible ability to switch themselves off and on.

Last year, visiting her mother in Paris, she had attended an opera at The Chatelaine. The work, Cherubini's *Medea*, was unknown to her, and rather than being bored and restless as she had been at previous like entertainments, Evelyn found herself sympathising, even identifying strongly with the sorceress. After the performance, her mother had opined, typically, that the original legend was patently a male fantasy/misconception concerning women. For, she had reasoned, who is more likely to kill their children when sexually spurned by their mate? A woman? No, a man. It was an established pattern of extreme male behaviour: men locking themselves in the family home, shooting the children and themselves, or gassing everyone in a car on their day of custody.

But though, from a view of social generalisation, what her mother had said was fairly inarguable, Evelyn still felt from the music and drama that Medea was credible, real, and that she herself could understand, perhaps even exonerate, a woman driven to killing her own children as the only means left to express her rage, and revenge herself against a husband she still loves and desires, who has deserted her for a younger, advantageous alternative. Yes, in the music and in her heart, she felt Medea's rage that heroic admired Jason could simply do this.

A rapid scampering cuts through the ambient noise of the storm, and Evelyn turns to meet the two gleaming brown eyes of a spotted-tailed quoll with chocolate bar, poised on her pack like a miniature statue. She flinches and it is out under the door. There is no way she can really stop the quolls coming in at night; they are obviously too used to campers. She will just have to make sure she leaves no scraps around and lock everything away before she sleeps.

Which reminds her she needs to eat. She doesn't feel hungry, possibly because she is overtired, but she stokes up the fire again and cooks up a vegetable curry which, once tasted, is greedily consumed. The break and meal refreshes, even lifts her, but soon enough she falls back to her brooding. She throws on more logs, and as night draws in and the cold sharpens, sits in a trance watching the voluptuous lick of the flames, coffee after coffee, dirty plates discarded in the dark.

Yes, the way a man can love a woman with only part of his mind is perhaps the most extraordinary thing of all. They seem to commit themselves, and then just turn away and become other beings with other matters fully in view. So presumably even while they are in the wildest throes of passion, somehow, somewhere all this other stuff is steadily ticking over like some bizarre machine. She catches their eyes in the train, on the street, desiring her, not caring about her, not even knowing her. Sex apart from personality, how is it possible?

It is now late and Evelyn realises she has worked herself into a state; a small drumbeat at her temples is a warning. She gathers up crockery, cutlery, pot and pans, ties them securely inside two plastic bags and suspends the bundle over the cooling ash bed in the fireplace. She will clean up properly in the light of day. Plenty of time tomorrow with this weather. Then she curls into her down bag, leaving on most of her clothes. Coddled in dry warmth, the storm raging outside is at first a comfort to her, but the wind howls strangely and she cannot find a comfortable position. The evening meditations run around unbidden, so clear, logical, undeniable. One particular post-coital exchange with Graeme keeps recurring.

Towards the end, again, a dreary wet Sunday afternoon in the group-shared terrace, the place empty for some reason, the two of them upstairs in bed. She is simply lying there, irritable, although the sex has been technically successful, listening to the rain, trying to let it soothe her. Normally he has the sense to leave her alone when she is like this, but this time he decides to tackle her. And as he begins, a nauseous familiarity flushes through her; he must have somehow learnt these lines from her former boyfriend, who in turn had somehow learnt them.

'I can't understand why you get upset like this. Why can't we just enjoy ourselves like other couples?'

'You can't understand, you don't know yourself. It's because you turn me into an object, as you fancy. I become your desire, and so I lose my self.'

'You're my girlfriend, Eve. It's normal to desire you. One would think you might even want it.'

'But not to reduce me.'

'Maybe in your way you reduce me.'

'To what?'

'An object of love.'

'Then you're not an object.'

'I exist because you love me. You love me because in turn you want to be loved, to be the most important thing in the whole world in one man's eyes, or perhaps in many men's eyes. And so where is my self in this?'

'Graeme, I give you so much.'

'So you might gain the controlling interest. Evelyn, if you're honest, part of you also wishes to lock me away for your own uses.'

'No! You're inadequate, so you try and make me feel inadequate.'

Over and over like the loop of a film.

A second day of enforced confinement. The storm has not let up and the rain has become snow: a white-out. The mercury has plummeted but Evelyn decides it is wasteful to light a fire for any but cooking purposes. She will have to get used to the cold anyway. She makes herself a light coffeeless breakfast, then rugs up and returns to bed.

Just sitting up in her bag, feeling low, staring down at the dirty empty hearth, listening to the endless wind. She considers getting her notes in some kind of order, sort out a preliminary structure, even just a loose categorisation, or read up more on the flora and fauna of the area, plan her trapping program. But she just stays there wrapped, her thoughts drifting aimlessly, inevitably always finding Graeme.

'Why do you have all these funks? Don't you ever ask yourself? Don't you want to try and deal with them, maybe find some way to get rid of them?'

'It's just me. Can't you accept that? If you love as you claim, you must love me warts and all, even in my blackest moods. I love you like that.'

'But Eve, I can't love you when you hate yourself.'

'That is such a weird thing to say. When I am at the worst, when I am in pain, that's when you should love me most!'

'But that's when you reject me. And then the only thing that lifts your mood is to hurt me.'

'Can't you see, only then can I begin to love you again, to accept your love.'

'When you hurt me?'

'When I can find a way to pity you.'

'When you feel I am beneath you.'

The hours drag on. She has finished with him, finished with them all. And yet at the time he seemed the one. She remembers how troubles in their relationship started appearing during the latter stages of her thesis. She was overworked and strained, at her most triumphant, and most doubtful. She had thrown all her strength and spirit, everything she had, into her work. To what extremes she drove herself to make it definitive, a model of its kind. And the benefit of that is she is here, part of this important study.

She makes herself get out of bed, has a sandwich and juice and at once feels revived. She pulls out some of the plastic supermarket bags collected in Hobart, and standing on the rickety desk chair, tries to stuff them, or part of them, into whatever leaking cracks she can reach. Surprisingly, this proves reasonably effective. When the storm passes, she'll climb on the roof and do a proper job.

Back in bed again, she looks around to see what other improvements she might effect. She muses how she has always been a perfectionist, an overachiever. She cannot divorce her perfectionism from anything, cannot do one thing well and shrug her shoulders at the rest.

Which is why her academic work has been consistently outstanding, why her fellow students envied, even idolised, her intelligence and energy. Her striving, her ambition seem things of such personal impulse and force. Like her famous mother, Evelyn Carter will make her own way, her own mark in this world, the old instinctual individual struggle. No, she could never have shared this hut with another scientist.

She further considers how through her concern to get every single thing right, she can easily lose sight of those odd things that really are important. This has been a problem in her study; she doesn't concentrate on areas of most weight, tries to learn it all and totally exhausts herself. So it is with much in her life. Surely it is an understandable, perhaps even commendable fault. Still, it is possible she might return from these three months with a huge amorphous mass of material with which she will need guidance. Which would be difficult to deal with, practically and psychologically.

Also her body, strong though it is, seems perversely to fail her at crucial moments. She just cannot cope when the headaches strike. And then her other foe, capricious paralysing doubt, always hovering in the background, and sometimes, like the headaches, overwhelming her, so that day to day living becomes a sequence of crises, each of which has to be separately grappled with and defeated.

Evelyn remembers how in these strained periods an enormous tension would settle on whatever was her current household and relationship, finding herself wondering at her fury over a dead pot plant, or the washing rained on, or an odd dirty plate. But then up to a certain limit, every relationship, household, family, perhaps every nation, generates its own peculiar roles, unique codes of behaviour, and one either accepts them or does not. Cohabitation or estrangement.

So she drifts on through the day, thinking about this and that, trying to use the time to work through problems about herself, about her future, until she feels she can go no further. Then she rises, finally allows herself to light a fire, which is magically warm and comforting, cooks a decent meal, and sits back staring into the flames trying to think about nothing at all.

When Evelyn wakes on the third morning, she has a headache. She takes some analgesics and checks outside. The weather has slackened but it is still too stormy to leave the hut. She forces down breakfast, then back to bed.

The clarity of her reflections of the previous days now seems muddied, her mind opaque. The pain is not acute, but there is that strange thickness that occasionally presages serious debilitation, and then finally the darkness. Lying there, staring at the roof, she has a persistent strange idea that she is painfully slowing down time, somehow using the weight in her head to grind it to a halt.

Late in the afternoon, all at once, the weather lifts. And so too, to an extent, does her pain. There is a pervasive ringing quiet; the storm has passed. Evelyn ventures out to see the evening sun beaming a sickly yellow light from an immense sky onto broad damp fields of snow. Over the padded land is a deathly silence like nothing she has ever previously experienced, as though the world is holding its breath.

It all looks extremely peculiar, especially through the thickness in her head. She has been confined with her broodings and now the landscape is transformed, just like when as a student she would attend an afternoon film, become totally lost in it, and emerge to find all mysteriously turned to night.

She knows the snow will melt quickly, probably by tomorrow, particularly if there is more rain. The front has moved through, which means she can finally begin her real work. It will be good to get out into the field, into the open.

That night she sleeps soundly and deeply, and when she wakes the snow has melted, the sun is shining bright and hard, and her head is blessedly clear.

Visiting

'I was a little concerned, Evelyn, with the weather, but none of the others have managed to contact me until today. And I know how experienced all of you are.'

'It was a pretty wild storm, professor. Up here anyway. Fortunately for me, it took a few hours before it really kicked in.'

'Everyone made it to their huts. So Roger will fly in today and make drops for three of you. You haven't had a chance to get back to the car, I suppose.'

'I'm walking down today. Tomorrow, I'll start work, I promise you.'

'Plenty of time. Good luck with it all. Joseph says you should pay him a visit if you get bored. You know where he's staying?'

'He showed me his hut on the map, and I've walked the area before. I'll keep him up my sleeve.'

'Good luck again. Look out for your dog, and keep in touch.'

'Sure. Thanks.'

Professor Atherton sounds warm and encouraging, even through the crackling ether.

Time to move. Evelyn assembles a minimal pack with some emergency provisions, including tent and sleeping bag, and heads off briskly on the long loop down to the car and back. The morning is crisp and clear. As she settles into stride, the first deep breaths of sharp air sting her throat and lungs, scour and fumigate her brain. So forget all this tangled man business, walk right away from it into a new world. Her joints and muscles limber up as she strolls free and easy under the solemn splendour of the pines, absorbing their authority and reverence. Yes, leave it behind, the pines whisper to her.

To start with a *tabula rasa*, like she feels this morning, is a fantasy she cannot help returning to. So much of her past life, with her mother, without her mother, with her boyfriends, only ever seems to her like something ugly and unnatural she should not have, travelling along with her like the pack, shadowing her, for all the world to see.

Still, striding high through the wilderness on this bright cold sunny day, surely she can push that stuff aside for a while. Live the moment walking. Walking: man's most natural activity, properly coordinating time to space. The long nomadic treks on the savannah, the pilgrimages central to every religion. Shedding the sins, shedding the baggage. Yes, this constant brooding has not been good for her, reappraisal notwithstanding. The headaches are the warning signs.

She inhales the mellow resin of the pines. Sunlight filters softly through the cool grace of the canopy and the blue shadows are all dapples of virgin snow. Her heart yearns towards these spotless badges. As she approaches the edge of the woods, bright light breaks through the foliage in solid shafts of dust and dew linking the green-shadowed world with one of harsher colour, in windswept bare contrast. On the ground, in these pools of sun, butterflies swarm, a seething kaleidoscope.

She walks up out of the trees into that light – Solomon's Throne blazes so she can barely look at it – then over Damascus Gate and a scramble down the slippery scree into the Walls. They rise around magnificent; she feels she is picking through the ruins of some vast cathedral.

The ground is marshy from rain and snowmelt so she hugs the high ground near the Western Wall. It is chilly in the huge shadow of the cliff and she moves on. Soon she is at Herod's Gate and pauses for the view and some biscuits and water. The sky is cloudless, the entire landscape has been rinsed by the storm, the colour of each constituent object defined and sharp as the object itself. She looks down across Wild Dog Creek up through the green expanse to the Jewels in the distance, then over to her left where she can see to the Cradle

Mountain range. The peaks are tipped with snow, and it will remain now for the season. It is a good feeling having Joseph next door, but it is also a good feeling, a better feeling, being here alone.

She hurries down to the creek and up to the Jewels. Another hour and a half and she is back at the car. It has not snowed below the plateau and is much warmer. Above, the weather holds, still no clouds. She turns the engine over. She knows she better take as much as she possibly can and loads up the pack to bursting, then begins the laborious journey home.

This is slow hard work. She feels fit but the ground is boggy in many places after the rain and difficult to negotiate with weight. Finally, in the late afternoon, Evelyn reaches the hut. It has been a very successful day's walk but she is done. For the past few hours, her calves and thighs have been stiffening up and her back aching dully. Still, she could not have done this a month ago. She dumps the pack on the floor and wanders around in a bit of a stupor, then shakes herself, lights a fire and brews some coffee.

Her damp boots smoke beside her, tongues and laces askew, as she settles close in to the growing flames. She stares at the bent air hovering above, stretching out and kneading her feet and legs, letting that radiant heat penetrate. The smooth skin over her firm calves shines red. Little hairs are returning after her last shave. Another thing she doesn't have to worry about in the wild. Men love hair on a woman's head and nowhere else. How bizarre. Hair, specialised scales. How she would love a massage, and a sauna. There's a good use for a boyfriend. Graeme had fine strong fiddler's hands, but it was his fiddle that got most of their attention. Hands that were gradually stiffening with arthritis.

And this is probably too much exertion for her for one day, at present anyway. She has to watch herself. With her will and spirit, she can push her body beyond the point of safety, and has on occasions. Sometimes when she is on a sustained walk through adverse conditions, she is hardly aware of how she is forcing herself. Her mind wanders off completely and her body labours of its own accord, like a thing apart. Tomorrow she will take it more easily, locate the drop and start mapping out the area. She cooks dinner, sorts through the new material, and turns in early and happy.

Evelyn sleeps heavily, yet is aware of her aching legs and back. At one point, her right calf bunches up in a cramp and she has to ease it out. Strange uneasy dreams drift through as though she is in a slight fever, and the wind rises as a descant to these. However, when she wakes, she cannot remember any of it but still is left with the feeling of something unpleasant lodged in the back of her mind, something pre-human down where the brain joins the spine. She is stiff and has difficulty rising and moving around the cabin at first, but after a while feels herself unfolding, loosening. And in a way she even enjoys the sensation of muscular ache; it reminds her of her physical self, her strong fit body. Another fine day, the first of real work.

Her initial task is to establish the rough boundaries of her study site, then make a detailed map of it. Before that, she must find the second drop of equipment and supplies. Since she can see nothing near the hut, she walks over to where she found the first drop and, sure enough, there are two large canvas bags tethered together. She lugs them back, has a quick check to make sure all is there, but decides to leave the actual sorting for the evening. Best to get out while the weather holds.

Probably easiest and neatest to initially concentrate her observations on the areas of the park most used by walkers, the region bound by the Walls and their immediate vicinity. If this does not yield an appropriate group of pademelons for her study, then she can extend it. To begin with, she will focus on a limited group of animals, but eventually she will need to reasonably establish what proportion of the general population has been infected by the lumpy jaw and project the consequences. From her readings of similar past studies, while in Hobart, it does seem that the immediate pademelon population here is slowly declining, but then this is virtually the case for all species. Lumpy jaw is a new, and possibly critical, element.

Also, as part of a general environmental comparison to the Walls, excluding the pademelons, Evelyn decides on a study of a small remote area that would not have seen walkers, a minor peak across the wasteland of the Long Tarns that stretch north-east from Mount Jerusalem.

Already in her mind she has divided the Walls area into specific geographical locations: upper plateau zones with woodlands, grasslands and heath, and high isolated peak zones with woodlands, heaths and rockfields. Over the next few days, she will look at each in turn, and then incorporate them into a general map. Since this morning she is physically tired, she will simply start off on her own doorstep, the valley and creek in front of the hut, which consists of open grass and low dense vegetation merging into a medium forest on the far side of the creek. She will gradually extend her range from this until she starts to tire.

Small white butterflies dance among the long grass stalks, impossibly fine single-thread spiderwebs netting the tips. Down on the dimpled surface of the creek, dragonflies stop and skim. As the morning warms, varied floral scents infuse the air. Evelyn shifts slowly around the area, which she assumes has seen some grazing by cattle, noting the degradation caused by erosion of tracks, how this has modified the vegetation, postulates how it might affect the wildlife population. The largest recent physical impact on the environment is the series of devastating fires that swept through in the early sixties. These have wiped out much of the pencil pine forest which is slow growing and having difficulty, particularly at this altitude, in re-establishing itself. The incidence of fires would have increased since the arrival of man, natives and Europeans. She wonders if the presence of walkers has retarded the growth of the pines, or if the loss of so many pines has changed the environment, the weather, the soil.

So she continues, entirely occupied and absorbed in her inquiries. She makes a few pencil sketches, then late afternoon wanders back to the hut and spends the evening working through the material from the drops, stacking the cages outside. She still has another drop to come. She will have to ensure she has everything she needs.

Next morning, early, she is up on the roof nailing down plastic bags under shingles where she identified leaks during the storm. She should really have done this yesterday, but the weather is holding and so she also manages to complete her limited reconnaissance and spends the evening after dinner drawing up a map by the light of an old kerosene lamp left in the cabin.

A leaf of flame burns calm and steady from the large braided wick, creating a mini solar system of bugs and moths, buzzing and flapping around the concave smoky glass in erratic orbits. Evelyn draws boldly and confidently with few corrections. Creating a spatial object like a map is also a great way to fix the landscape in her mind. It is work she knows and likes. Collecting data, analysing it, processing it; using her training, the money and hope invested in her talent and skills, to make a small but real addition to the vast sum of human knowledge.

Being a zoologist, she naturally is most interested in the impact of environmental change on the wildlife, particularly the pademelons. But she is mindful to give due regard to other aspects, broaden the value of her work. Her work in Hobart under the professor will prove handy, plus the few reference books she has lugged up, including a constant travelling companion, a battered beloved paperback of Darwin's *On the Origin of Species*.

How stimulating to extend her range of inquiries beyond the zoological, take on Joseph's naturalist manifesto, minus the politics. A deeper insight into how the total environment interacts, its complete and complex dynamic. She plumps out her notes with a quote from Darwin: '…the woodpecker, with its feet, tail, beak, and tongue so admirably adapted to catch insects under the bark of trees. In the case of the mistletoe, which draws its nourishment from certain trees, which has seeds that must be transported by certain birds, and which has flowers with separate sexes absolutely requiring the agency of certain insects to bring pollen from one flower to the other.'

She thinks of Joseph's metaphor of dialogue. Perhaps he is right, and something like the fire, for example, is an instance of dialogue being radically disturbed, even broken. Of course, as Darwin himself continually points out, underneath all the harmony or dialogue, or alongside it, there is also fierce clash and competition. Evolutionarily, greater forms have only been created through adversity. And in every instance more individuals are produced than can possibly survive, including presumably, human beings.

The next day is another one of heavy physical labour: placing and setting the pademelon traps. From her map, Evelyn has traced out traplines along the interface of the wooded and open areas. She places them in groupings five metres apart, plants in each an apple in the back smothered with peanut butter and a drop or two of vanilla essence. Then she covers them with large plastic garbage bags and pins them down and, for this first stage, ties the trapdoor up. The animals can come and go as they please.

Keen to get them all done, and with the weather still fine, she overworks herself. She retires early, as she must rise at dawn, but her head is racing and she cannot sleep. At first she worries over this, then decides just to lie there and forget it.

The distinct and particular voices of the night. She is not aware of drifting off, there is simply a sense of time passing, but suddenly is brought to by the rattle of cutlery outside. She sits up, groggy. It is cold. What if it is the dog again? Should she go out and investigate? The rattling stops. Her illuminated watch dial says two-thirty. Rising quickly, she pulls on her parka and ventures outside with a torch. There is nothing around, but the plates have definitely been disturbed. Might have been possums or quolls, or even devils. She returns to her sleeping bag and lies awake in the dark. The creature or creatures do not return.

At five in the morning, moving around the traps by torchlight through a low freezing mist, Evelyn examines each of them carefully. Some are undisturbed and some show possum interference, most have had the apple taken. She naps during the day and checks the traps again the following night. There are more apples gone. Now she sets them properly, with the trapdoor cocked.

Another twenty-four hours and she makes a good haul: seven pademelons, three with bad lumpy jaw, one with a moderate case, and three completely clean. She allows the moderate to escape. For the others, she fits a hessian bag over the mouth of each trap, blows on the animal from behind so that it hops into the sack, and then tags it on the ear. On these three clean and three infected she fits a copper collar with a transmitter, and also a green beta light.

Now she has her group, the real study begins. Resting as much as possible during the day, she tracks each animal three nights in a row. It is heavy and cumbersome work. In addition to her protective clothing and emergency pack, she carries a radio receiver, which she uses to dial into the particular animal's transmitter frequency, a three-pronged aerial, a spotlight with a spotlight battery, a headlamp strapped to her forehead and, tucked into her belt, a map, compass and binoculars.

After each three-night stint, exhausted, she gives herself a break for a day and night and writes up her observations, then she repeats the exercise. Each animal has individual features Evelyn quickly comes to recognise. Initially she names them C1, C2, C3, and LJ1, LJ2, LJ3, but LJ3 is a friendly old male, seemingly suffering more than the other two diseased animals, probably due to his age, and so she gives him a proper name, Henry, after a grizzled stray dog she once adopted.

All three of the infected animals show the telltale hard swellings on their jaws and faces and subsequent weight loss, but Henry also has pus discharging through breaks in his skin. Such an advanced stage of lumpy jaw invariably means that the infection has spread beyond the soft tissues, muscles and tendons into the bones, osteomyelitis, which puts Henry beyond any individual curing, if such a thing were possible in these circumstances. Although he must be enduring a moderate level of pain, he seems to go about his business much as his fellows. She is reminded of the dignified stoicism of beasts.

The morning after the fourth batch of surveys, Evelyn finds herself unable to gather her thoughts and write up her notes. Listless, she knows what she needs to do, but her ideas are scattered and she has no control over them, no will to work. A pot of strong coffee only seems to make matters worse, for although her mind is buzzing, she cannot focus through the haze, and now has a slight headache as well.

She decides on a walk out to the car, a break in routine and change of scenery. There are still some notebooks and supplies she needs to bring in, and light mindless exercise might help dissipate her nervous energy.

The day is overcast with a thin high cloud cover, dully bright, glary, but there is no wind and the sky looks steady. Evelyn takes only her daypack to prevent herself loading up too much, and finds she handles the round journey well, despite her tiredness. On her return, the uniform cloud descends, the peaks are obscured, tendrils of mist penetrate the valleys, and in the final hours she has to push against a persistent light sleet.

The weather seems to be closing in again; she is grateful to arrive back at the hut merely damp and cold. As she walks through the half-open door, it strikes her immediately. The smell. Cutting through the familiar odour of cold woodsmoke is an overpowering smell of an animal. A large male animal.

Then her pack. The strongest pack she could afford has been ripped open, cleanly, from where it is still hanging on the wall. Foodstuff is spread all over the ground, though not much has actually been eaten. No possum or devil could possibly have done this. The big dog has been here, right here in her hut! She shivers involuntarily and closes the cabin door firmly, fixing it with the large rock she has placed there for that purpose. Stunned totally, momentarily she is paralysed by some inexplicable horror; then she is all panic and wild activity, placing everything back as quickly and correctly as she can, sweeping away all signs of the intruder.

Pausing, the smell catches her again and nausea sweeps through her. She must air the place, expunge the odour. Dragging back the rock, she opens the door, and when the cold wet fresh air hits, her stomach heaves. She races outside and retches violently into the grass.

Over and over she convulses. Despite the wind and sleet, sweat pours down her face mingling with her tears.

Finally, she rests back on her haunches, panting, totally done, dazed, little spots contracting in front of her. What has happened, what really has happened here? The dog or whatever it is has got in, that is all. Nothing more. Perfectly natural. And what has she done? Acted like a total lunatic. The footprints. She staggers to her feet, wincing from the pain in her gut, and limps frantically back to the hut. Yes, to her horror she has cleared them all up, not one sign. The only prints in the faint residue of flour that remains are her own. The prints would have settled everything. She pulls out one of the books Bob Baines has given her on the thylacine. She stares down at the open page at the prints of a large male. She cannot trust her memory on this, particularly in such a state.

Suddenly she is weeping. She's acted like a juvenile; possibly botched a great zoological discovery. She could have photographed them. They were clear, that much she does remember. Then she sits down and calms herself. Realistically, it is almost certainly a dog. And after this she will most probably come across it again. The immediate task is to finish clearing up, and get something in her stomach if she can. Then she must lie down and rest, and hopefully, eventually, fall asleep.

The pack presents a bit of a problem. It is not ruined completely; the animal has torn it just once, but almost ripped off the whole front. The synthetic material is extremely tough. She can fix it to some extent with fishing line she has brought specifically for pack repairs, although she hardly reckoned on anything like this. From now on, it will leak in the wet, and she will have to replace it when she returns. This dog must have very powerful jaws. And again – no, maybe for the first time – Evelyn is genuinely frightened, rationally frightened. She is no physical coward, she knows, and it is a very odd feeling, this particular disquiet. She has never experienced it in the bush before.

Still, it is highly unlikely the creature will attack. If it is a domestic dog, she is confident she can handle it, and even if, fantastically, it is actually a thylacine, there are no known instances of thylacines attacking men. On the contrary, they had a reputation for docility. She is considerably larger than a wallaby or sheep. Nevertheless, after this little episode she must keep her door firmly wedged closed at night, and also when she goes out. Take her camera with her, always. And maybe a knife.

Haunted again by her nemesis, the wind, she has a sleepless feverish night, and next morning is still highly agitated. She cannot work like this. She can walk out and drive to Hobart and the professor and return with some help, but then her whole project here might be irretrievably compromised.

Or alternatively, she can trek over to Joseph in the Cradle Mountain area. She can contact the professor but she doesn't know Joseph's number. She could ask the professor for it of course, but she would still prefer to leave him out of it for the present. It's not that serious, surely. So, if she is worried, perhaps go and see Joseph, respond to his casual invitation; it is not such a long way. No sooner does she fix on this idea than it suddenly seems like some kind of lifeline. She can discuss the incident fully with him, unofficially; he's reasonable and practical, he'll have an idea what she should do, if anything.

Fortunately, because Joseph is a keen fisherman, another practical outdoor skill he possesses, he has made his temporary home at a hut almost halfway between the two parks, at the southern tip of large dammed Lake Rowallan, accessible by car. From the maps, he is only ten kilometres due west as the crow flies from Evelyn's own hut. However, the flight of the crow for her on land is a difficult and dangerous route, involving a trackless descent from the plateau. Much simpler for her to walk north back to the car, drive out of the park, and then south along the dirt road adjacent to the lake to where it ends, half a kilometre from Joseph's hut. Five hours walk to the car and a nine-kilometre drive along the Mersey Forest road which might take an hour. Twelve hours round trip plus time for a chat should present no problem so long as the weather holds. She could start now. Perhaps it is a bit of an extravagant effort for what might amount to only a twenty-minute conversation, but she really needs to get away from the hut, from the smell, from the whole damn business.

A light pack and she's off and at once feeling better. Some hours later, the car is waiting patiently like a reliable friend. Starts first twist; the drive will do it good. She gobbles down some scroggin and stale water, and three-points out of the narrow clearing. The well-graded state forest road is a dull drive, plenty of depressing evidence of government sanctioned devastation, no view of the lake until the very end. Here she finds the familiar rusty E.J. with its faded wilderness society stickers. She pulls in next to it, and heads north on foot following a path that crosses a shallow creek running out of the lake.

Before she is mentally prepared for it, Joseph's hut is before her, smaller, more modern and ramshackle than her own place, cobbled together with bark, wire and corrugated iron. There is a makeshift clothesline out front with a few items. She recognises the T-shirt; probably his whole wardrobe is Wilderness Society stock. Seeing all this, she gets cold feet. She considers turning around before he notices her. He is probably out in the field anyway and she can leave a note. That would be easier, although hardly solves her original problem. She's come all this way after all.

Advancing cautiously into the clearing, she ducks under the line, the clothes are still dripping, and knocks sheepishly on the heavy awkward door. A shuffle and it swings inward to disclose a partly dishevelled Joseph, wearing only a pair of khaki King Gee shorts in the cold shadow, blinking at her in mild surprise.

'Oh, hello, Evelyn. Everything all right?'

'I was at a bit of a loose end, needed a break from work.'

'Sure. Right. Good to see you.'

'I've been to Cradle Mountain before. Was quite interested to have a look at the area again.'

'It's another hour into the park proper.'

'I know. Probably won't do it this time. Just checking the lie of the land.'

He has a little medallion around his neck. She can't help staring at it.

'I'm allergic to penicillin,' he explains.

'I don't want to disturb you or anything.'

'I think I'm pretty much up to date with my correspondence and phone messages. Come in. Excuse the mess.'

'Thanks.'

She follows him gingerly into the little room. Same smell of woodsmoke and tamped earth, much smaller and cruder, but the room also looks a lot cosier, warmer. A lozenge of honey sunlight rests on the floor like a natural inmate. She stands looking round, feeling out of place and wondering how with much the same objects as she possesses, he has created such a different world, a better world she thinks. He has even tacked a homemade curtain to his single window, a somewhat feminine touch that has also eluded her.

Her eye catches four sizeable fish strung on a line, the opal sheen of their slick forms glinting dully in the dusty light over the fireplace, which is stacked tidily with boxes and cans. So he just relies on fuel, like a responsible camper, not that there would be much wood around here, and it wouldn't get as cold either, not yet anyway. The fishing was another good idea; plenty of fresh food always at hand.

'You'll have to sit on the bed. I'll light up the stove and we'll have a cuppa.'

'I don't want to waste your fuel.'

'I've got plenty, and more back at the car. Despite what the professor might have told you, I like my creature comforts, particularly for a long stint like this.'

'Me too.' She dumps her pack on the bed and sits beside it, relaxing a little. She stretches, without the pack her wet back is cold.

'Cooked food, tea and coffee. I've even got a bottle of brandy and some joints. My fellow purists would not be impressed.'

'Things are Spartan enough anyway.'

'Absolutely. You'll have to take some fish back with you. Had a lucky day yesterday.'

'Thanks. I will.'

'I was thinking the other night how you must have walked in during that big storm. Did you have to bivouac or anything?'

'No, I just made it. Bit of luck, bit of willpower.'

'Bet you were happy when you walked in that door.'

'Yeah, but I was snowed in for some time.' She watches him balance a saucepan precariously on top of the small stove.

'Creek water's fine,' he says, seeing her watching him. 'I don't worry any more about boiling it or anything.'

He hasn't really asked her why she's come. Perhaps her lame excuse is sufficient. Perhaps he doesn't care, pleased like she is now for a little company. He shuffles clumsily with the enamel cups and saucepan, though presumably he has performed this particular action so many times he could do it blindfolded.

'It'll have to be black. I've no milk, I'm sorry. Don't drink it.'

'Another allergy?'

'You make me sound like a hypochondriac. I like to boil up my oats with water.'

'Black's fine. You got any sugar?'

'Sure. One?'

'Thanks.'

He moves over and squats opposite her on an old oil drum he must use for a desk. He is close, their knees are almost touching, and she can smell him; he hasn't washed for a while, but even though this isn't fresh sweat like the morning of the plane, he still smells good. Maybe it is the wilderness, because he smells to her a bit like an animal. There is something else: yes, surely he smells very slightly like the beast. Or is it her imagination? No, definitely. Here it is not repelling. Why? Because he is her species.

He hands her the mug holding it by the rim, ignoring the pain. 'I am a bit surprised to see you. But it's nice to have a chat with someone.'

She brings the drink up, inhales the sweet steam. It is impossible to put her lips to these things with boiling fluid in them. Even the handle is hot. Metal mugs, what a stupid invention.

'So,' he says, 'how's it all going?'

'Fine,' she answers, and as she says this, she realises she is not going to tell him. A wild dog has invaded her sanctuary. So what? She can just keep the door closed from now on. What does she expect him to do? How can he give her better advice than she can give herself? She just got a fright, overreacted, and then what does she do? Run to the nearest bloody male! Christ! What would her mother think? And does he think it odd her turning up on his doorstep out of the blue?

The silence between them now hangs heavy upon her. But he is staring into the rising steam of his mug with no air of expectation whatsoever.

'As well as the dope, I've got some tobacco if you want a smoke.'

'Thanks. I don't smoke.'

'I need something out here when there's no company.'

'I tend to drink coffee.'

'Hypes me up too much.'

'I'd just thought I'd like to take a look around, at where I walked before. Made quite an impact on me.'

'It's beautiful country.'

'I'm a bit restless, I guess.'

At this, he looks up at her and she feels herself colouring slightly. Has he caught a false note?

He has. Joseph accepted her explanation as to why she has shown up without question, but now she repeats it to him, for some reason he thinks it isn't quite true. Then why is she here? He dismisses any romantic possibility; she couldn't be that interested in him on such slender acquaintance. No, something else is going on. Why does he think that? Just because she is on edge? But she is an edgy person, and restless, as she says.

'Anything you need over there?'

'No, I think I'm pretty right.'

'Just ask.'

'Thanks. I will.'

'But you will take some fish.'

'Of course. Love to.'

'So do you think you'll recognise where you walked?' This is inane, he knows, but just like at the restaurant, he senses she isn't comfortable with silence, unlike him, and needs him to help her fill the gaps.

'It's funny how you take it all in,' she says, 'ninety-nine per cent of my life I cannot recall a thing, but two weeks in the wilderness years ago and I can remember every detail, one after another, like little episodes in a long film.'

'It's so intense because the other ninety-nine per cent is all the same. I've spent lots of time up here and I don't remember it all like that. Odd moments of course.'

'Have you started working yet?'

This is a slightly unprofessional question, not that he cares.

'A little. I'm not so good at writing. Tend to put it off, happier out in the field. You would've got a bit done during that storm, I guess.'

'No. I had a bad headache for those days.'

'That's no good. Do you have some Panadol?'

'It's more serious than that. I've got special prescription drugs. It's a chronic condition, on and off.'

'No fun being cooped up with a headache.'

Which is probably the explanation, in addition to what she says. Company. A break. She'd probably need to get away and talk if they were as bad as that.

'Do they debilitate you much?'

'It's all right. I know how to cope with them.'

'As you can see,' he says 'I'm not so far. I'll give you my radio number. If you get ill at all, need any help.'

'Thanks. I'll keep it in mind.'

He writes out a number on a scrap of paper and hands it over. 'If there are any real problems, don't hesitate. I mean it.'

'Thanks for the cuppa. I might get going now. Make the hut before dark.'

Then she's not going on any further, he thinks. Why did she suggest it? Covering tracks.

'The weather's fine,' he says. 'I like camping out occasionally. For a break. Here, I'll get you those fish.' He unhooks a couple from the line and wraps them carefully in greaseproof paper. 'They're gutted. Careful not to crush them.'

'I will. Thanks a lot. They look delicious.'

'They are.'

'It's been good to see you.'

She sounds likes she means it.

'Likewise.'

She shoulders her pack and walks out into the sunlight.

He follows close behind. 'I mean it,' he repeats. 'Just call me. What about that dog you mentioned?'

'No sign yet.'

'Okay, have a good walk back.'

'Thanks. Good luck with your work.' She waves, then quickly walks away without looking back.

He watches her departing figure, enjoying the movement of her long legs and bum in her stretch ski pants. He's pretty sure she's lost weight. Could just be the exercise. But he still feels disturbed for some reason. She was more than just on edge.

He goes back over their conversation. With conversations, particularly between men and women, there is more often than not another silent one being conducted. Surely this was the case here, although he is equally sure it has nothing to do with romance. But definitely, she came all that way from the Walls to tell him something, in person, something that has happened to her that presumably she doesn't want to tell the professor. Just what was that thing?

The Hunt

Evelyn arrives back from the now familiar route at eight. It is almost dark, and already the sun is setting much earlier. One of the fish lightly pan-fried with margarine, onion and pepper tastes like a restaurant meal, but even after the cooking there is still a faint trace of the beast in the air, or is it just the memory lodged in her olfactory glands? It was a good idea seeing Joseph, even if she decided not to discuss this problem with him. She is in considerably better spirits than this morning. If she changes her mind, he is always there, and now she can contact him via radio.

Late next morning, she wakes from her first good sleep in ages. The smell is still there, giving a claustrophobic atmosphere to the cabin, the oppressive heaviness of a distinct other presence. Male glands. While working through the morning at her notes, she leaves the door open to air. In the late afternoon, she makes herself lie down for an hour, even though she is not in the least tired, as that night she will be tracking.

After dinner, the second fish. Evelyn again applies herself to her notes, still feeling fresh, and just before midnight dons all her gear in preparation for the long dark hours ahead. She makes her way across the stream and climbs up the opposite bank to a prominent spur. She will give herself a bit of a break tonight and follow Henry as he ambles painfully around his feeding area. Trying his transmitter frequency, she immediately picks up a signal. Fortuitously, he is just below her, near the hut, and moving slowly in the direction of the pine forest. She descends and follows him into the enclosing depths of the forest, where there is no residual light and she is completely reliant on her headlamp and Henry's steady beep. It is important to try and keep back a good distance from him so as not to disturb his usual foraging habits. Evelyn settles down into her routine, vital data for her project, but cold and boring work.

As always, she feels how eerie and unsettling it is trailing a disembodied electronic signal through the night. The dark falls around her like a heavy blanket, and it is this perhaps that triggers an increasing restlessness, and a curious strain in the work itself, the source or sources of which she cannot initially fix. Since his movements are normal, she assumes Henry is either unconcerned about her, or given his illness doesn't even know she is following him. An unnerving fantasy settles on her, with a growing persistence, maybe partly in reaction to the boredom, that while she is tracking she is also being tracked, a conceit that once established, makes it difficult for her to give sustained attention to her quarry and her work.

She has occasionally experienced this somewhat paranoid but hardly unnatural sensation on previous tracking nights, but for some reason tonight it is more powerful than she has ever known it. Perhaps it is simply her surrounds: the low creeping mist, the dense chilled air, the unseen but imagined presence of the great gloomy forest canopy casting her into a sort of underworld, one seemingly peopled by the ghostly trunks and wild frozen limbs sequentially caught in her roving headlamp.

It is not these effigies themselves that seem to be spooking her, as they did previously, but something that seems to lie behind them, or beyond them. She switches off her receiver, and then her headlamp. Utter pitch. She feels extraordinarily vulnerable standing there blinking blind – a diurnal domesticated mammal completely out of its element – but she hears only what she knows to be the usual night crepitations. The occasional rustle of possum, quoll and bird, the various small creatures of the night going about their businesses. The faint background trickle of an icy stream.

She tries to tune herself into the inky darkness, the subtleties of the living forest, much as she has tuned her receiver into Henry's frequency. Let herself feel finely, be actively passive, perhaps even discover and develop senses other than her customary overused five. Or further sensitise her five, attempt to attain the smell and hearing of a wild thing.

Beasts smell like we see, all those subtle tonal gradings, but there is a dimension of time: they also smell what has been, as though you could look at a scene and see its past, and so perhaps guess its future. And they can hear all those higher frequencies, the silent dog whistle… She recalls a Victorian ghost story she once read about a man who finds a silent whistle in a ruin; he blows on it and unknowingly summons up a malevolent spirit.

Nothing she can fix on, but such a powerful feeling. She wonders if something is following her or, more probably, if she is creating this 'something' for some reason with her peculiar complex of fancies and fears. Is she somehow, then, tracking herself? If so, what could it mean?

She switches the headlamp back on, swings it around erratically, focusing on the varying perspectives presented in the beam by the random placement of the ancient pines. Nothing. She must get a hold of her nerves and get on with her job, proceed through the routine just as she has on previous nights, just as she must on successive nights.

This Evelyn forces herself to do, but at some personal cost. Henry spends the rest of the night in the pine forest, therefore so does she, unable ever to shake off the firm conviction, without any proof, that all the time she is being followed, just as all the time she is following. A little before dawn she walks out and returns to the hut, considerably shaken, although the night has been fine and still, and she has collected good data on Henry's nocturnal feeding range, which she can usefully compare with that similarly compiled from the other five study group pademelons. It has been a long night partly because Henry is a far less efficient forager. With his advanced disease and age, it is becoming increasingly difficult for him to simply sustain himself, a struggle that must shortly defeat him.

Back inside the hut, Evelyn's anxiety dissipates, but she still feels as though she is under some kind of peculiar spell. Exhaustion, presumably, although she doubts whether she could sleep at this point. Some muesli and coffee help cheer and warm her, but the dreamy sensation lingers. Everything she touches seems slightly unreal, every act she performs, supernatural, either with a strange déjà vu tinge or alternately a feeling of predestination. Whenever she stops moving, it is as if she is somehow still in motion. All sights and sounds and smells seem more vivid, even though, paradoxically, experienced through an enveloping gauze which, like a theatrical scrim, creates a sensual chiaroscuro.

Sometimes it is like this for her before a bad headache. A sort of silver-tingling light euphoria, although at present there is no accompanying background heaviness. She was also like this, she remembers, for days as she completed her thesis; it was when she wrote her most brilliant and difficult passages. She was inspired. And recalling that, suddenly she is filled with a nervy energy and feels intolerably cramped by the damp room. The air is thick and slightly rank, soupy; all metal surfaces are wet. Maybe the dense humidity is why everything feels strange, and also why it is so very silent. Opening the cabin door, she peers out into the grey twilight, raw with cold. The sky is clear, a few sparse stars linger faintly. She slips her boots back on and tromps down through the sodden grass to the creek.

Before her is the bulk of Mount Jerusalem, silhouetted sharply against the pre-dawn sky. Maybe she can scurry up to the top before sunrise; the east is cloud-free, it is a good opportunity. She takes a few deep gulps of the freezing spring water, returns, grabs her parka, sashes it round her waist, and heads off.

Happy to be back out in the biting air, and without all her heavy night gear, she climbs quickly and confidently up the rocky slope, skirting the tarns, not sticking to any path, leaping recklessly from boulder to boulder and pushing through the tough scrub. She feels reborn out of the long dreary night, alert and elate. Ascending is easy and pleasurable, she is almost floating up, climbing with the strange ease of a dream, immune to cold and exhaustion like a god. Although, as the going steepens, she starts to flag, slows, even pauses for a moment to examine some beautiful red lichen and catch her breath, but it is not long before she is standing triumphantly at the summit.

The wind is bracing, and although she is now sweating, Evelyn wraps her parka around and raises the hood. She will be cold shortly. The eastern horizon is significantly lighter than the sky but there is as yet no distinct glow. The view is fine nevertheless. Gazing north-west over the lakes country, towards the departing night, the long stretches of water are soft and silver, fading with the forest into the grey distance. Now she is still, the dreamy sensation, spell, again manifests. Perhaps it has never left her.

A flickering movement at the base of her vision diverts her attention. Almost directly below her over the steep eastern wall, is a wide U-shaped valley formed from sheets of clay, poorly dried acid soils supporting sedgeland, bogs and stretches of wet heath. The flat level ground and a bolster plant community, mostly cushion plants and alpine coral fern, impede any water flow. The valley was probably once a lake and would quickly fill again in heavy rain.

She scans the landforms. Nothing. No, there it is: a pademelon, moving quickly, very quickly, almost as if it were being pursued. It is Henry! Old, sick Henry showing amazing dexterity, scampering erratically, frantically, hardly bothering to avoid the pools and bogs. He looks exhausted and terrified. She peers in the general direction from where he has run, south-west down the valley back towards her hut. For a while she sees nothing. Then her focus is caught, as in a trap.

It is at a distance, but if this is a dog, it is a most peculiar dog. Still too far away, and there is not enough light to see whether it has the distinctive stripes, but what makes it immediately different from any canine is the tail. The tail is very long and does not appear to move independently from the body; rather it is an extension of it. The beast is moving slowly, almost skulking, but with purpose. She reckons it about five minutes behind her pademelon. It cannot see its prey, it is scenting a trail.

She returns to Henry, taking a few moments to locate him. From his present condition, Evelyn assumes the pursuit has been on for some time, presumably just after she left him. So her instinct had probably been right: it had been trailing her trailing him, waiting patiently for her to leave the scene. The persistence of the hunter. Henry presumably had not known then, either about her or about the beast, but after she had left, the beast closed, and Henry's instinct kicked in.

She returns to the beast, which is steadily approaching the area beneath her vantage point. If it follows the pademelon's path exactly, it will pass directly beneath her at a distance of a couple of hundred metres. Now the sky is notably lighter. She should have a good view. But she does not have her camera. And after she had told herself.

She sticks steadily to the beast. Its gait is also different from a dog's, a sort of trot; occasionally it breaks into a shambling canter. At one point it stops and raises itself briefly on its hind legs to scan the terrain. This action is like a dog, but still it is no dog, that she can now see clearly. She looks carefully around it in a wide sweep to see if there are any others of its kind, but it appears to be a solitary, stalking its prey, slowly running it down to exhaustion. The kill, if it happens, will probably occur out of her range of vision.

Henry has changed direction slightly and is heading more westerly. She looks back to the beast. There can be no doubt about it. A thylacine, Tasmanian tiger, long believed extinct except by a few recalcitrants. She can now see plainly the stripes running down its rump and onto the butt of its tail. How maddening not to have a camera, but the shot would not be a good one, one of those particular set of conditions where the naked eye has immense advantage over a camera lens.

But with any luck she will see it again. For like all large sole carnivores, thylacines would no doubt have a specific territory and it obviously hunts and feeds in this area. Also at present there are no campers around to disturb it, only herself. She follows it intently, confirming the identification with every passing second. Yes, despite lack of camera, this is a momentous sighting.

Back again to Henry. He has changed direction once more and is moving almost due west. Now she remembers: when macropods are pursued, they run in wide circles; it is not known why, perhaps some kind of homing instinct. The thylacine has stopped and is rising up and down on its hind legs again. The pademelon runs over a small patch of high ground and she sees the tiger spot it. It falls to all fours and quickens its pace, then sharply changes direction to its left, trotting off the trail. Now they are in relatively open country, it is cutting across the chord of the pademelon's slow circle.

The sun rises behind her, she can feel it on her back; the first light limns the mountain peaks and flanks with a pale yellow. She turns round briefly to see the endless stretch of inhospitable rocky tarn country to the east catch the oblique raking rays.

Both creatures are moving away from her, across towards the other end of the pencil pine forest, between the Temple and Zion Hill. Maybe Henry is trying to make the shelter of the trees. The exhausted creature is still a good distance from the forest and it looks to her as though the tiger will cut off his trail well in advance.

Moving along the diagonal, the tiger has made up ground efficiently and the pademelon is obviously unaware of the trap being set. In another few minutes, the tiger is ahead of Henry's path. Now it slows and sniffs around, making sure its prey has not passed. Then it places itself on a large flat rock with some bushes for cover, and waits.

The animals are close to a kilometre distant, but Evelyn can still see the drama plainly. The tiger has made a slight miscalculation. Henry will pass north of its position. But the tiger sees him again. It creeps carefully off the rock and stalks through the low scrub. Henry, though exhausted and presumably in considerable pain, is, she estimates, still moving more quickly than the tiger can run. If he makes it past the tiger this time and into the shelter of the forest, he could well save himself. The tiger can pursue him through the forest, but there visibility is restricted compared to this open valley and it might give up the chase.

The tiger closes in steadily. It looks as though it has timed its move well. Barring accidents, it should reach the pademelon before the latter reaches the trees. She loses sight of the tiger. It is down low, using a small rise of ground as cover. She watches Henry. On he runs, frantically, sensing violence close behind, in fact now in front, slowly circling towards the trees and possible safety.

He ducks behind the small rise where she has lost sight of the tiger. Nothing. A few minutes. Still nothing; neither creature emerges. The tiger must have made its kill. She waits another ten agonising minutes. Still nothing. She carefully notes the position of the place in her mind, levelling it up against a few other landmarks she will not mistake, then bolts back down the mountain towards the cabin to grab her camera. If she is really lucky, she will make the kill – if there has been a kill; no, there must have been – before the tiger has finished. And even if she doesn't manage it, she must get to the site before the inevitable devils clear up all traces.

She runs down heedlessly, down seems longer than up, arrives at the hut breathless, grabs some chocolate and her camera and sets off. In terms of distance, she only has a couple of kilometres to cover, but the ground is boggy under the long slippery dew-freighted grasses, and it is one maddening hour before she arrives at the area sighted from the cliff. Another twenty minutes before she finds Henry's corpse.

The tiger is gone and crows are on the scene. Evelyn throws a couple of stones and they flap away heavily, reluctantly. She examines the body. The ribcage is crushed completely. This is probably where the tiger has initially seized the creature, breaking the chest open with its powerful jaws. The innards have been consumed, heart, lungs, kidneys, liver, and the rest left for the devils and other scavengers. This is consistent with descriptions of kills in Professor Baines's notes, but at that moment, with the fantastic sequence of preceding events, it seems to her to have a voodoo quality.

She takes a couple of shots, then searches around for footprints, but finds nothing; the immediate ground is too rocky and hard. There is no indication where the tiger has gone. All reports on kills by the thylacine concur that the creature only eats fresh meat and never returns to a kill. Efforts by farmers and early settlers to poison the tiger with tainted meat invariably failed. There is really not much point in her hanging around. The devils will quickly polish off the remains. It would be better to slowly backtrack on what she assumes to have been the tiger's path to see if she can find any fur, prints or scats.

She is back at the hut about two hours later, having found nothing further, but still wildly excited. She writes down everything she can possibly recall about the sighting. She considers calling the professor at once, but decides to wait. What she really needs is a photograph, or photos of footprints, or fur. Something, anything tangible. Otherwise she's possibly just another fantasist. She is clearly in or near the tiger's present immediate territory. Her best chance of seeing the animal again and perhaps getting a shot of it is to stay close, not bring anyone else in, and remain vigilant.

All right, if she has not seen the tiger or any further sign of it in a fortnight, then she will inform the appropriate authorities, and a proper search can be mounted. For the present, stay still and quiet. She will retrace the approximate route of the kill again in the afternoon. And conduct a thorough search of the general environs over the next couple of days, weather permitting.

She is now certain the tiger was following her at night. Was she in its way, or was it using her as stalking horse? She is easy to locate in the forest at night, and the tiger knows she is tracking pademelons. She will have to stop. By now she pretty much has sufficient data on the six animals for her study needs, and anyway the cold is beginning to be a deterrent. She can work with what she has got and see how she goes.

Evelyn sets off again to the site of the kill, this time slowly and deliberately. She arrives back at the scene towards dusk. With the fading light, the devils have appeared and eaten even the bones. On her appearance, they scamper off. Now there is only a scrap of fur and some dried blood on the ground, which the ants have also found. What effective cleaners the devils are. Maybe one of the reasons a tiger never returns to its victim.

Back home, she tries to think of ways to attract the tiger. She could leave food out at night among the cutlery. She doesn't have any more meat. Maybe it would like cheese. It has come sniffing around once before. Perhaps she can hook up the camera to some sort of trigger or something. She thinks about this for a while, but can't really see how it can be done. Nevertheless, she leaves some cheese and bread out that night when she takes out her dirty cutlery. If she can get the tiger into the habit of snooping around, then sooner or later she will get a good shot of it.

Despite having missed an entire night's sleep, Evelyn lies awake in her sleeping bag, far too thrilled to drift off. She pictures it all in her mind time and again, particularly the hunt itself, repellent and yet fascinating like any violent drama. It was the hunt above all that primitive man ritualised, even aestheticised in those amazing cave paintings. Magic and art. The hunt was man's most vital way of bonding with the forest and with his fellow. Blood bonding, occasionally incorporating human sacrifice. Propitiation to the natural world, life for life. It seems to her, lying there in the dark, that within such a community there could be nothing more sacred, mysterious and moving than that particular fatal consummation.

Again she falls unknowingly into sleep to be woken by the rattle of cutlery. She sits bolt upright in her sleeping bag, her heart beating furiously. The plates clatter. Something is moving around. It is there, she is certain, the thylacine, just a few feet away through the wall of the hut, breathing the same air she is breathing. Rising as quietly as possible, she dons her parka, attaches the flash to her camera, and creeps outside. As she opens the door, something scampers off, a lighter sound than she supposes a tiger would make. Her torch shows only scattered plates. She walks over. The food she has left has all gone. She will repeat the exercise.

But the next night, after all the excitement and late hours, she sleeps soundly, and doesn't hear whatever comes and eats the food. She misses it the night after, and after that. It is simply too cold for her to sit up outside all night. Since she tracked Henry, the night temperature has been dropping below freezing, and there has been a thick sugary crust of frost on the ground each morning. She could pitch her tent and lie awake in the sleeping bag. That would not be too bad.

That day, after the usual routine of field studies and writing, she has a nap in the afternoon, then erects her tent with the fly facing the area where she usually leaves the plates. After dusk and dinner, she sets herself up with a coffee Thermos and sleeping bag and camera at the ready. And waits.

It is a quiet fine night with a little moonlight but, with the front tent flap open, bitterly cold. She wears a balaclava but still her nose runs. Despite this, close to the ground and with partial loss of vision, all the scents are much stronger, particularly the damp earth, and also the bitter bracken which seems to hold odd floating wisps of mist to itself jealously. At her face, brilliant patches of new grass shine with a hard metallic lustre, beyond the clearing the masses of foliage are indistinguishable. The time ticks by very slowly. A little after midnight, a large possum appears and noisily devours the food. Predictable, but she still needed to know.

It is almost a week now since she saw the tiger. That might be the only sighting she will obtain, and she might have to rest content with it. Still, it was a great event and the creature must be around somewhere. Whether she sees it again or not, sooner or later someone, a scientist or a hiker, will sight and record it, she is sure. But then what will happen?

Consciousness

The sky shuts down; blustery cold days, thick and woolly grey. When Evelyn pauses in her work, she can feel that cold through the soles of her boots. No further sign of the tiger; perhaps it has moved on. Shrugging aside the pervading gloom and a predictable deflation after all the excitement, she again settles into her professional routine, observing and writing, sometimes late into the nights, by the kerosene lamp and the fading glow of the fire. Once fully back into rhythm, she feels fine, although there is always the nagging worry that when she becomes totally wrapped up in a project, as she always does, it is difficult for her to tell just how well she is progressing.

She stifles the occasional outbreak of concern over this by reassuring herself it is still relatively early days, and anyway it is reasonable, perhaps even necessary, that she allow a little leeway for error and waste. She has demanded so much of herself in the past, but she has accomplished what she has partly because of this. Then again, she must also learn when to demand, how to save her greatest energies for greatest use.

After considerable wrangling, she has changed her mind on the tiger and decided to tell no one what has happened here until she is finished. She tries a few random dawn watch-outs from the top of the mountain without any further success. Thinking it through again, she realises that, unfortunately, there is simply no hard evidence to back her sighting, and her work in the park is important, both for the environment and her future career.

As the days pass slowly, absorbed by work and lone musings, Evelyn increasingly finds herself a prey to strange varying moods. Sometimes she seems to go about taking notes, rinsing clothes, dicing vegetables, as if in a trance. Most notable of these recurring states is a sort of rapt natural holism, something she knows from her general reading is not uncommon or unusual for solitaries in the wild.

And indeed, she welcomes these particular communions as long sought-after balm for her city-chafed soul. Perhaps they are even crucial in her gaining a fully comprehensive understanding of her surrounds. A growing spiritual empathy can only help make her work and time here more worthwhile.

One blustery morning she is slowly skirting the pebbled shore of a small lake. The gusts off the troubled surface are freezing, and after a while she takes refuge amongst a dense grove of wind-bent pines, a secluded retreat where the water has seeped through a fissure in the rocks in a gleaming thread to open out into a little pond.

Here the sheltered surface is entirely still, and amongst the tangled sunken roots of the old trees, delicate bush flowers silently lean into their own reflections. She fondles their petals idly. Flowers, lovely to our eyes, but different to the general green only so they might attract birds and bees, although of course there is a complicated link between these creatures' instinct here and our aesthetic pleasure.

The enclosure seems so complete, so intense, it is like a living thing itself, with its own meditative spirit. The intensity is partly one of contrast, her awareness that outside is an enormous open vista. As Evelyn looks around and settles into the place, it casts its particular spell, and the rapt mood possesses her.

So important to be reminded that wilderness is not only heroic windswept plains and vertiginous crags, it is also separate still spots like this where one can open out the self in complete peace and solitude, like these bush flowers. For although, she considers, it is a common-place idea among writers of the natural world that everything in the wilderness is also within us – that nature's various forms can present to the mind types of its desires – this idea is not really made manifest, until finally one is in the wilderness, hearing, seeing, smelling, touching these very strange, very familiar parts of ourselves. She places her work down beside her, and gazes across the silver skin of water. It all looks so perfect.

Which brings to mind a sentence from the last pages of Darwin's *Origin* she has always found troubling: 'And as natural selection works solely by and for the good of each being, all corporeal and mental endowments will tend to progress towards perfection.'

That our world evolved at all can sometimes be reasonably understood, at other times appears a miracle, impossible really to grasp the immensity of it. It is Darwin's word 'progress' that disturbs her. It reminds her of Graeme's idea of simple protoplasm, through almost unimaginably gradual and complex processes, eventually becoming great teeming cities.

The primitive and the untouched seem far purer, much closer to her ideal of perfection. For right here, it seems, casually enfolded around her is a surviving fragment of the original pristine world, Joseph's Gondwanaland, a little Eden, a sanctity preceding religion, preceding man. For perhaps somewhere like this, she further muses, is possibly where it all began, amino acids somehow transmuting to the first water-born cells of life. And so she has returned to the metaphoric source, as anyone can, to then later re-enter the sick populous city, like a holy pilgrim bearing crucial messages of life and faith.

Just as from another like 'cell', somewhere in central Africa, primitive man stepped out of the primeval forest, proud and erect, onto a limitless savannah, an empty unknown fearful space that he had the guts and brains to make his own. He stepped out to eventually populate and also pollute the entire planet, and so finally, bizarrely, begin to swallow his own tail like some giant suicidal snake. Pride, the original sin, the denial of Nature's essential democracy.

For (rising now on her imaginary pulpit) once man conceives himself apart from Nature, walks away forever from vital replenishing sources such as this, once he believes he has full knowledge of himself and knows himself superior, it is necessarily the beginning of the end.

For her, that is the meaning of the myth. This is how we have exiled ourselves from Eden, willingly breaking off from the chain of nature, assuming the role of God, and thus we are damned.

For even our own individual beings are in many ways little complete evolutionary worlds. As, for example, the foetuses of fish, man, bird all have gill slits and tails, so man, so all mammals, in their foetal development sketch the entire history of their race, are a living metaphoric history of the natural world. And are a natural world, an interdependent living system, but at the same time vitally dependent.

She settles against a commodious trunk, her mind beating on. Civilised man, pathetically watering his confined domestic patch of green, or playing golf or swimming laps, or chewing himself up in a tiny room like a caged monkey. So far have we travelled down this damned trail, so degenerate is our living, that now the wilderness is most precious because it is apart, because it is different. The wild fenced off, fenced in, so we can access it selectively, dip into a vital part of ourselves. Man has split his brain in two, killed his own brother, his better self.

At this last thought, a feeling of great bitterness sweeps over her, leaving in its wake an actual physical residue, a sharp metallic taste under her tongue.

She tries to clear her mind, force herself away from these thoughts and back to the healing balm of the grove. For here she is, in the wilderness, the real thing, and she is sure nothing has disturbed, or ever probably will disturb, the limpid surface of this lovely pond while it endures, nothing except the decay of these flowers. But this idea, when she dwells on it, for some reason begins to fill her with a curious disquiet, a thing very different from the angry indignation she has just felt.

The world ever growing and decaying, places of beauty being created, lasting for who knows how long, and then being destroyed, probably violently, their existence unknown. The inconstancy, the evanescence and the energy expended, what does it mean? One day her own passionate frame will be scattered to the wasting winds. Is her deep love for the natural world as purposeless as the changing changeless world itself? She is down again. Too much brooding; she needs activity.

Evelyn gathers up her things and walks back out into the open. The sun emerges from behind a bunched muscle of cloud and the morning all at once expands, her eyes smart and her mood again lifts. For the first time in many days, sunlight lies around her in a profligate abundance. More than that, the very air itself now seems bright as if with a presence, a joy. But then at this thought, for some reason, a shadow again falls upon her.

For now, after all her thinking, she does not feel a component of the wilderness but rather an alien object within it, one destructive man, enemy agent, cancer cell. Further, that the wilderness is conscious of this, not antagonistic exactly, but wary. Out here, the wilderness is watching her. She stands motionless, exposed, listening to the wind, catching a faint echo of its unearthly night keening. The plains and valleys are empty no longer, the wide air embodied, the wild as aware of her as she is of it, and for a few fraught moments the tension between them both seems intolerable.

Is the wilderness passive as she so blithely assumes, or might it possibly in some way be active? Even arrayed against her? Here it is in all its brave and baffling aspects, all encompassing, all powerful and glorious, and here she is single, alone. Man the enemy, wandered unthinkingly from the security of his camp across the border.

The stress of this presses down on her head, like the sunlight, and all at once she wants to cry out: it is not her fault if she does not fit in, because she so desperately wants to, needs to. But how say anything to silence, non-response. She can literally cry out of course; with sufficient rapture, she could even perhaps become her cry.

If she does break out in such a manner, it might entail that the covenant she believes she has so carefully, painstakingly, established between herself and Nature over the weeks will be broken, even irreconcilably. If she cries out against the wilderness, attempts to publicly stake out her difference, or protest at perhaps being different, it might simply turn its back on her. Or it might respond malevolently.

Slowly, slowly, she dampens down the impulse.

And to lose control like that, even for a moment, would also be a considerable blot on her own personal prestige, or even the thin edge of the wedge. Wedging open what? She feels her fear rising again, something outside as well as inside, like a grip on her throat.

For while it is surely no revelation the wilderness is watching her (no doubt it has been watching her ever since she came clumping into the park), hearing her, feeling her, what if it has decided, for whatever reason, that she is superfluous? Then she will need somehow to be got rid of, expelled. Maybe the big storm, for example, was some kind of test. But she endured that well enough, heroically in fact.

What is happening to her? How can these beautiful spaces remain a joy if she feels she is being watched like this, eternally anxious for no good reason? She can never recall feeling this way before in the wild, thinking like this. Not at Cradle Mountain, not in her long stretches in the Blue Mountains. Always she has felt safe and composed. Something else must be going on.

All at once, the answer leaps at her, as though it has been crouching and gathering all the while, even during the quiet time of the pond. It's not the wilderness that is watching her, although of course that has been happening in some low-key way all along. It is the tiger.

All her varied impressions of the morning suddenly crystallise, clarify, as if under a sharply focused lens. That is what she has been really sensing all along, for days, why she has been so unsettled. Now she can home in on it, undeniably it is the same presence she felt in the forest that fateful night when tracking Henry, or at any rate, the same feeling.

Because she doesn't possess the acute sensitivity of a pademelon, a wild thing, it has taken that much longer to register, and for her to work it all out. The further divination of that crucial night in the forest, that extra sense. Now, all at once, she is preternaturally aware. The tiger, his eyes on her right as she stands here. She cannot see him, but he is here. He has been watching her since she first left the hut this morning, stalking her in a way, although presumably with no intent of attack.

The wind drops away and there is an extraordinary stillness. The air is throbbing, electric. She feels incredibly exposed, apprehensive, even fearful, but also, strangely, she has never felt so alive, so centred. For it is peculiarly thrilling, in a way, to be the sole focus of attention of such a rare and magnificent beast, so fully worthy of its interest. That extraordinary sighting of it through the morning mist. It is a distinct privilege. The tiger sizing her up, and maybe on behalf of the wilderness, as its chief representative.

It strikes her what a ridiculous idea it has been of hers to search for the tiger, look out for it, for surely such an animal must always be more aware of her than she could ever possibly be of it. It would be watching her whenever she is out, considering what she is about, and most particularly why she might want to find it. And in consideration of this last, presumably what to do about her. For just as in the broad way she was debating the wilderness's intent, the tiger also must eventually come to some decision concerning her, and then respond. Most probably if it finds her a nuisance, it will simply avoid her. But she is on its territory.

Bob Baines told her there had been no recorded attacks on man, that the animal had a docile reputation. Still, it is a large carnivore, and it is certainly not docile to pademelons. It can attack when it needs or wants to. Maybe the hut invasion is really a warning. Get off my property; trespassers forbidden.

Her fear is rising again, but more substantial. Fear with a known object. She is out here completely defenceless. Not even a knife. She must return to the hut immediately.

She begins to walk back, steadily, keeping to open stretches, trying not to betray from her gait that anything is out of the ordinary, that she is perturbed. She forces her gaze forwards, resists the continual temptation to look around and behind.

But a beast of the wild like that, so attuned, must know she knows, and also know she is scared. Still, surely it is important to display her nerve. Courage, dignity, these are qualities all beasts respect and admire.

After a tense hour, she reaches the hut without incident. No creature has attempted to enter it or been around as far as she can tell. She secures the door with relief. The cold air inside clings to her and she realises she is soaked in sweat.

She changes her shirt and boils up a saucepan of water for some tea. She watches, fascinated, as a column of silver bubbles rises as if by magic from the aluminium base. She knows she can walk out and return to Hobart. Joseph is not far and can offer her general support and advice, but he can't really drop his own important work and help her here, and she can't expect him to, she's been over all that. She contemplates telling him, but has no photographs, has nothing. What if they return and find nothing? It would be unendurable. She would look a complete fool and all her good work here would be irretrievably compromised, ruined in fact, and probably her future as well.

She must stay and brazen it out; there is no alternative. The tiger has not approached her. It is most logical to think it disturbed the hut that one time for food. She has not really begun seeking it out in any serious way. Just lying out one night in a tent watching possums. She is not threatening or harassing it, competing for its food. Maybe it just needs time to get used to her, and she to it. It needs to see she is no threat. She must carry on as normal, but for the present best to stick to open areas for her work. And carry a weapon. That scimitar she souvenired at Maria Island, no doubt it has seen service. It only needs cleaning and sharpening.

So, armed with this barbaric oddity, Evelyn forces herself to once again venture out into the day. From the sustained charged state of the air, she still feels she is being watched, everywhere she moves, but she sees nothing definite, and eventually she is able, apprehensively, to return to her observations and field notes.

In like manner, the next few days and nights continue. Thankfully, she does begin to relax somewhat; after a while she can go about her business almost as normal. But now that she knows the tiger's eyes may be upon her at any time, and probably at all times it senses where she is and what she is about, she always carries the convict knife.

Contact

'I just called to see how you were going.'

'Thanks, professor. No problems.'

'We agreed last time you would call me Monday, remember. I was in all day, so I just assumed you were busy.'

'Yes, that's right.' The note is staring at her from the calendar she has hanging from a nail on the wall.

'Joseph mentioned you paid him a visit. So, as I said, I just rang up to see how you were going.'

She needs to feed him a bone. 'I'm sorry about Monday. As I said, everything's fine and, what's more, I've come across some further signs of that animal we were discussing.'

'Animal? So you still haven't identified it as a dog. What kind of signs?'

'Professor, I believe it's possible that it might be a thylacine. But I need to obtain highly compelling or even irrefutable evidence, good photos, prints or fur or something like, before I start making any claims. I'm sure you appreciate my professional credibility is at stake here.' A pause. A big formal mouthful, but she means every word.

'Evelyn, I don't want to put you in a difficult position, but what are you saying to me? You have had further…what? Actual sightings?'

'One.'

'Was it clear?'

'Clear enough.'

'Why, that's marvellous!'

'But I have nothing substantial, scientifically. Please, for the present, I don't want this to go any further than just between us. I promise to keep you fully informed of any developments.'

'I'll leave it all in your undoubtedly capable hands. Well! And everything else is really all right? Health?'

'I'm fine.'

'You've still got another drop in three weeks' time. I'll speak to you before then of course. Ring me two weeks from today. Think about anything extra you might need.'

'Sure.'

'I'll be looking forward to your next report with considerable interest. Take care.'

'Thanks, professor.'

She is convinced it was a tiger, but every year many feel the same way about similar sightings, including, occasionally, professionals in the field, and not one of those claims has been verified in almost half a century. She is right, she knows, but she needs more, much more. Again, she argues, that would be the worst scenario: her returning and reporting the sighting, as she knows she is duty-bound to do, and absolutely nothing eventuating except considerable cost and dashed expectations. Well, she will just have to hope for more. In the meantime, she must try and largely put it out of her mind, and get on with her project work.

One mild morning finds Evelyn in a mossy valley cupped with sunlight. The state that possessed her before the drama of the kill has come upon her. She has fought it for an hour but now succumbs, settling dreamily into a comfortable nook. With the sun on her face and no breath of wind in the air, time drifts by. Her mind is nowhere.

She idly, somewhat compulsively, starts rubbing the convict knife with one frayed edge of her flannelette shirt, admiring the rough but sure workmanship. She would like to be as this knife, keen and purposeful. The blade momently dazzles her and she glances away up to where a creek is trickling down from under a large boulder.

Something. Nothing.

The colours of the landscape, the planes and patterns, seem like those trick one-dimensional abstract sheets occasionally found in show bags or children's books, that if held at a certain distance while allowing one's vision to shift out of focus, magically resolve into a startling three-dimensional image. She relaxes her eyes in just this way, and there, standing on the boulder, motionless, is the tiger, not more than fifty metres distant, its head slightly to one side, regarding her quizzically. She sees how it is the exact shade of the foliage behind it.

The animal does not move, or react to her seeing it. Evelyn cannot shift. One moment the world is at ease, then suddenly it is gridded with tension. One moment the world is this valley and the surrounding plains and mountains and far-off cities and oceans; then it contracts to her and this beast, their set eyes and the charged connecting cord.

Ageless minutes pass.

What is it doing out here in the middle of the day? Is it an old animal, last of a dispersed population, seeking easy food sources such as carrion before the devils get to it? Or has it just woken up to have a look at her?

They continue to stare at one another, and rather than feeling rooted to the spot, Evelyn now begins to experience a strange weight-lessness. She reaches a point of uneasy calm within herself, when the tiger moves. She seizes up again, but the beast merely settles casually down onto its stomach with its head erect and alert, like a dog. It now looks less threatening, but it still keeps its eyes steadily on her.

This movement of the tiger's shifts her slightly back to reality. Shortly she must do something. She must decide on how she is going to act, then act in the way she has decided. But there is no harm in staying still a little longer. Let it get very used to her looking at it, meeting it equally. Now she observes it carefully. It has long whiskers and a head like a dog, but the ears are shorter and rounder. She thinks the rounded ears in a way make it look quite cute, very marsupial.

Evelyn knows animals can watch and wait motionless for hours, but she cannot. Gradually she rises to her feet. No reaction. She is stiff and finds it difficult to stand. Slowly she hoists her pack. The tiger watches her. She searches through the pack and finds her little Olympus Trip camera. She places the pack back down, carefully lines up the shot and takes three. The tiger responds by yawning, revealing an extraordinarily wide gape and a healthy set of fine, sharp teeth. She freezes again. Those are the same powerful jaws that crushed a pademelon's ribcage and easily ripped open this same pack on her back.

As if in response to her imagining its various acts of violence, actual and possible, the animal places its head down on its paws with a docile sleepy expression, and observes her through half-closed lids. She has to admit to herself that this wild carnivorous beast, at present, appears pretty relaxed. But then again, animals are always alert, an imperative survival condition of the wild, and they can snap into determined, planned action at once, even from deep sleep.

Evelyn sidewalks, backtracks, very slowly, deliberately towards the ridge of the valley opposite, away from the tiger, moving by chance also in the direction of her hut. Eventually, she reaches the crest of the ridge; she must take her eyes off the tiger for a moment to scramble up onto the rocks, and when she turns back round, it has vanished. She tries the focus trick again, but it is definitely not there.

From this vantage, the valley is entirely open to her. She scans the terrain minutely, takes her time until she is reasonably certain that there is nowhere the animal is hiding, despite its natural camouflage. In all probability, it has simply become bored with her and walked off.

She decides to return to the hut to compose herself in a safe place, so that she can then build up the courage to return to this same spot. She needs to make what the tiger, if it is still around, will perceive as a natural territorial demonstration. She needs to show that this is one place where she customarily moves, tiger or no tiger. She must overcome her fear and locate herself as a normal object in the tiger's environment, relatively new but of no particular account.

Evelyn hikes back to the hut, all eyes, seeing nothing. It is one o'clock, her usual lunchtime. She forces down some biscuits and cheese and coffee, then gradually screws up her courage and convinces herself of the necessity to return to the valley.

She gathers her gear, opens the door, and the tiger is there, crouching barely ten metres away. It has tracked her. This time she feels more in control. The door is right behind. She slips her pack, brings out the camera and knife and starts snapping, her heart knocking against her ribs. She advances a step and at this, the tiger rises up on its feet languidly, shakes itself and moves off down towards the creek. She notices how awkward it looks when it turns, which it does all in a piece, like a ship, but it jumps neatly from rock to rock over the creek, before trotting up the other side of the valley. It climbs quickly among the crags, and then it passes out of sight, behind a clump of high bushes near the top of the ridge.

She waits a while but it doesn't reappear. She looks up across the valley, then further up the opposite cliff into the sun and she sights it again, standing on a high rock ledge about a kilometre away almost at the top of the cliff. In that position, poised between her and the sun, on a natural focal point up over the entire valley, the animal seems to Evelyn almost to assume a numinous power, like some mythical emblematic beast of bygone ages. It yawns again, emitting a high-pitched yapping sound, with the second yap lower in pitch like an echo. Then it trots over the top of the cliff and out of sight.

She has seen three times, twice at close quarters, the Tasmanian tiger, maybe has even shared a few moments of its company. Now also she has photographed it. When she returns to Hobart, her story will be a sensation and she will be famous, her career assured.

She shakes her head in bewilderment. It is difficult for her to fully grasp what has occurred, so deep the significance and so wide the possible consequences. She cannot tell what is going to happen from here but everything has changed. She considers leaving, but no one is going to come in until she tells. The longer she stays here, the greater the chance of more sightings. If she does not see the tiger again in another fortnight, then she will leave.

An amazing thing has happened to her. She has been stressing over her relationship with the wilderness, all the potential antitheses, but it is also possible that despite them, the wilderness has taken her to itself after all, even chosen her. Will she be betraying this privilege by leaving, by telling? This is something she must resolve in her mind before she is finished here. In the meantime, as always of course, there is her set work.

For eight days, Evelyn sees no further sign of the tiger. After the encounter, she finds it a considerable trial to maintain a steady focus on lumpy jaw and hiker degradation, and their somewhat more mundane ramifications. On the other hand, this work is still important, it does help keep her mind diverted, and it is good she must be occupied. Each day she is gradually progressing with her project, building up a useful written record and portrait from all her observations and tentative deliberations.

But then one morning, when she is wandering aimlessly through the landscape, she looks up to find herself again back at the isolated grove of pines and perfect little pond where she experienced such a powerful intimation of unseen presence. And that same sensation of being watched steadily steals upon her .

She walks out of the grove as she did before, to clear her head, and suddenly there it is, amazing, just the same, the thylacine squatting on its haunches on a ledge thirty metres away, again regarding her lazily. Once more, she freezes. Minutes pass and, as before, nothing happens. She looks at it and it looks at her. She does not move; nor does it. Slowly, keeping an eye at all times on the tiger, she gathers her gear and again takes a couple of shots. Then she begins to back away, always watching and with one hand on the knife.

When she has walked a few yards, the tiger abruptly leaves its rock and follows her. She keeps moving and it keeps following. She stops for a couple of minutes, and the beast settles itself back down on some other comfortable vantage point to continue observing her.

Evelyn begins to become alarmed. What if the tiger is tracking her like the pademelon? Although it is not hiding itself at all, or moving up on her in any dangerous manner. She is still a distance from the hut and she cannot outrun the animal through the bush. If it does want to attack her there is nothing that she can do except fight it. Best to try and stay cool and calm, not appear frightened, and just as before make her way quickly and unobtrusively back home.

With nervous deliberation, she walks on, always keeping a close eye on the animal, which follows continually at a discreet distance. Rather than the tiger tracking her, after a while she begins to feel, strangely, as though she is leading it on some invisible leash, and also even more strangely, as though in some way she is also being led. The set space between them seems enchanted. Finally, she reaches the hut with no further incident.

Evelyn locks herself in for an hour. When she ventures outside the tiger has gone, and she does not see it for the rest of the day. Nor the next. But the day after, exactly the same thing happens: the tiger appears, and when she walks away it follows her, always maintaining a set distance. Once more she returns to the hut and locks herself in until it has left.

The following day when this is again repeated, Evelyn attempts to appear to ignore the beast and pursue her work, always watching it out of the corner of her eye and keeping the knife at hand. But the tiger just tags her placidly. The next day as well. It seems that the creature is simply curious of her and means no harm. She considers that she is a rather big animal in its eyes for it to attack, and anyway there is an abundance of game around.

'No, professor, no further sightings. No positive proof.'

How could she possibly tell him what is happening? She can barely believe it herself. What if the photos don't come out, or are unclear? She will tell them, she will of course, she has to, she knows, but not yet, when she comes out, with hopefully more.

'What a pity! Well, keep at it. Now, as I said before it is a worry to me that you are late with this call. I've tried to call you a couple of times without success. You must try to remember to call me. It's important Evelyn.'

'I'm sorry professor. I just get involved with my work.'

'The last drop will be in a couple of days. Anything special you need?'

'No. Toilet paper, fresh fruit and vegies, some frozen meat and long-life milk. I'm basically down to my cans which is also what's left in the car.'

'No problem. Remember, call on time, and I'm always here if something unexpected happens.'

'I know. Thanks.'

Day after day the tiger seeks her out and moves along with her, constantly, laying a peculiar pall of tension over her field studies. These she persists in, with a kind of wild bravado, each day out, despite the animal's presence. The only alternative is to quit the park and this, for the present, with these further sightings and her uncertainty as to what they might mean, she has set her mind against.

Gradually, she begins to become more accustomed to the tiger's presence; still the tension never lifts, never can while she is being observed in this manner. One morning the tiger is actually waiting outside her hut, waiting for her to emerge for her round of work. It follows her the entire day. And the next.

A few day later she is taking a lunch break beside a deep clear lake, back against a rock wall in the sun watching her now constant follower watching her, when the tiger starts to walk up towards her, casually but deliberately. Evelyn tries to scramble to her feet, but again she finds she cannot move. There is not much room for her to move anyway. In fact, initially, she thinks she does move and finds she has not, as in a nightmare. That's when she knows her will is broken, her proud will, and that the tiger is transfixing her, a creature of greater power. Still, the knife is in her hand, and she is certain, if it attacks, with a superhuman effort she can overcome her trance and fight it.

The tiger comes right to her, stopping about a metre away. She looks into its eyes. So close. They are strange, like the wilderness, but then there is also something familiar and trusting. It turns its head on one side, quizzically, as it did on the first day she saw it after the hunt. She can smell it now. Slowly, apprehensively, with one hand on the knife, not even knowing why she is doing such a thing, who is directing her, Evelyn half rises to her knees, and with her other hand slowly reaches forward.

She watches her hand moving across the charged space, as though she were watching a thing disconnected from herself, a thing she has no control over, and she recalls Darwin's observation that the hand of a man has a framework of bones similar to the wing of the bat, the fin of the porpoise, the leg of a horse. Yet that hand, with its opposable thumb, its complicated possibilities of movement and manipulation, has led to the formation of a brain which has made all the difference in the world between man and those other beasts. And this beast as well.

She touches the tiger very lightly on its head. It makes no response. She brings her hand back and smells the odour of its hide on her fingertips, rubs the invisible layer of slightly viscous oil between her pads. She recalls the smell in the hut. Something momentous seems to be happening here to her; she cannot comprehend what it might be, but for some reason can apprehend its significance.

She leans forward again to pat the creature softly between its ears, through fear and tension with something like the clumsy delicacy of a child. It likes this, for it pushes its head up into her hand, just like a cat or dog. She pats it again and it nuzzles against her. It makes no attempt to bite. It seems to be perfectly docile, even tame. Then she moves closer and strokes its greasy flanks and it grunts in obvious satisfaction, and comes up beside her and settles down with a small satisfied sigh.

Evelyn is astonished at the ease and familiarity of the situation. Here is the rarest large mammal on earth, for decades believed extinct, submitting happily and naturally to her caresses, even inviting them. It seems a bit like finding oneself unexpectedly having an intimate and friendly tête-à-tête with a famous celebrity or head of state.

The tiger closes its eyes and starts to doze beside her. She picks up the notes she was making before being interrupted and attempts to work as normal. Her hands are shaking. Slowly she masters herself and continues to write in a stiff cramped manner. The tiger now snores lightly, and twitches its ears and flanks like a dog dreaming. Evelyn finishes what she had set herself, lingers a while, then packs up and starts to move on. The tiger wakes at once and tags closely.

The next morning when Evelyn emerges from the hut, the tiger is again waiting for her outside her door. The morning after, it comes bounding over, rising on its hind legs like a dog to be petted.

And so, like the days since the first mutual contact, it keeps close to her, a seemingly constant, faithful and affectionate companion. Somehow, Evelyn does not know how, without any effort on her part whatever, in fact with some aversion, she has tamed and befriended the rarest beast in the wilderness. Or has it tamed her? She finds it all utterly fantastic, but in due course she learns to almost relax with the tiger around. She has to, for it never seems to leave her alone.

Then it disappears for a couple of days. She frets and is unable to work. But one morning it turns up, apparently exactly the same, and from that time on, except at night when she sleeps and the tiger presumably hunts, it is always in Evelyn's company and will not leave her alone.

So arises, over a period of several weeks, that somewhat odd, but certainly not unusual or unnatural, open and relaxed companionship that can develop between man and beast. For some reason, the tiger has decided to adopt Evelyn, seemingly completely. Somehow she has become, or so it appears to her, a part of the creature's life.

And in due course, alone in the wilderness with her studies and her musings, the tiger gradually becomes in its own particular way, as other animals she has known and owned and loved have been in their time, a part of her life as well.

Insomnia

Evelyn lies in complete blackness; she sees, hears, feels, smells, tastes nothing. Now her mind might be the only thing left in the world, it might even be the world. For when she is caught in this drift of perpetual darkness, how can she know it is not?

She hears the wind start up, leans into its distinctive voice, and is both comforted and frightened by the conviction that in some indefinable but undeniable way, the wind speaks to her of a world beyond. And she can feel her heavy down bag coddled around her. She had forgotten that, lost the sense of it. She seeks out the edge of the zip with her cheek. It is cold and scratches her, has a distinct metallic taste and smell. She opens her eyes to the dim contours of the hut.

These signs infer a world of which in truth she knows but the slightest fragment, and one that presently she cannot approach except with unreliable memory. But focus on this memory, on the wonders of the world she has known, and turn ordinary belief into faith. She must have faith in the tiger. Not simply because it is the most wonderful thing in the world that has happened to her, but because it has somehow become the keystone, supporting the entrance to the edifice and therefore the edifice itself.

From nothing to faith. The tiger is a miracle, and so it has made her special. Not only because it is special and she is intimate with it – that is only reflected light like the moon – but because of her vocation.

Always she has wanted to be a zoologist, because always, even as a little girl, she has loved and been fascinated by animals, especially warm-blooded intelligent animals. They have also loved her in return.

Animals are beautiful, surely this is the first thing. Every living thing, including man, has its own particular beauty, although some creatures are more obviously beautiful than others. She cannot tell why, and it does not really matter; what matters is the force, and beauty is a force, a power, undeniable as the wind. Because it cannot be rationalised it is often discounted, explained away as some by-product of a certain culture, dependent upon that culture for its meaning.

When Evelyn is first attracted to a man, for whatever reason, she never thinks him physically beautiful, even if her friends tell her he is, or even if she can clearly see that he is. Then, as she knows him, as the relationship progresses, she gradually begins to think of him as solely beautiful, above everything else, his eyes, his legs, his wrists. She comes to know his beauty inwardly.

This is different to her reaction to landscape, which is immediate. Perhaps with men her guard is up, and their beauty slips beneath. Graeme had a fine, slight body, not a shred of fat, all burnt off by artistic tension. His talent was in his mind, but also it was there in his fingers and hands and wrists, and in the supporting veins and tendons. You could see it and touch it. She thinks of Joseph's body. Also no fat, but stockier than Graeme's. A strong, broad chest and thick muscled thighs.

She thinks of the tiger. She was frightened of it at first, but fascinated. And no matter what her fear, even when she briefly thought it might be stalking her, she knew she must be drawn to it.

The tiger's beauty, like almost any animal other than man, seems obvious. But then that beauty has also grown like the beauty of a man. As her knowledge of and familiarity with the tiger have increased, its beauty has developed, deepened with intimacy. She is now beginning to know it individually, in the same way as she has known the beauty of individual men such as Graeme. As day by day she has noted in her journal in precise detail the tiger's specific physical characteristics, each one of them, and the composite, have slowly become charged with a relevance beyond the merely scientific, beyond her professional disinterested interest.

Initially she naturally compared it with a dog. Since Evelyn left boarding school, she has owned dogs and knows dogs well. But almost immediately she began to notice all the ways in which the tiger differed, to see how it was unmistakably unique. The stance, how the neck and front legs are fairly short, and how powerful the back legs are by comparison, how the tail is long and rigid and cannot be wagged.

It still amazes her how the tiger lets her handle and examine it freely; more, it has grown to expect this attention, basking in the sun, grunting in satisfaction as she strokes it, half on its back, front paws bent slightly in supplication.

She pictures the detail: the body hair short and dense and the fur on the tail tight and close, again unlike a dog, and the ventral belly hair lighter in colour than the rest of the body, a lovely creamy hue. Then there is the odd continuation of the body stripes onto the butt of the tail, conveying the impression that the tail is an extension of the body, once again unlike a dog. How she loves to stroke its firm flanks, the fine pelt hot from the sun, the extraordinary muscles beneath, taut and alive. But most of all she loves to fondle the soft round ears, and the tiger has come to enjoy that especially.

Evelyn is a little warm now and rouses herself to toss off her top layer, her unzipped sleeping bag. She considers making herself a drink. Some milk or herbal tea might help her sleep. She would like to fall asleep, but it is not unpleasant lying here. She is floating contentedly and if she rises, the mood might be disturbed.

She slept well last night, and if she does not sleep tonight, tomorrow will be tiring, but then she will work with the satisfaction, confidence that she will sleep the following night. Still, a drink would be good.

She sits up and lets her head clear. Wriggling out of the bag, she dons her parka, grabs her torch and takes a few unsteady steps towards the fireplace. The coals are still warm and she stokes up a modest blaze. She heats some powdered milk and cocoa in a saucepan, takes a mug back to the bag and sits leaning her face into its steam, sipping it slowly, feeling it warming her gut. She places the mug on the shelf behind her, snuggles back down and, closing her eyes, reaches for her last thread of thought.

The physical beauty of an animal is never a static thing, a museum thing, it is not a quality that can ever be caught and held, even by the closest observation and finest writing. The magnificence of a beast is neither for the delight of man, nor for man's comprehension and appropriation, it is part of an environmental function. And so this beauty is most powerful when manifested in action, showing its true reason and being. For Evelyn, the tiger greatly increases in beauty, fascination, when occasionally giving notice of, or even displaying, that terrific energy that she knows, even when it is in repose, is always coiled within.

That first sight of the tiger tracking and killing the pademelon made an indelible impression. Time and again she has replayed the incident in her mind. In the dawn light, interacting so fully with Nature, the tiger had revealed its most profound physical and spiritual glory, and from this first climactic event she attained an insight into the beauty of its species, a generic beauty.

Australia's primitive mammals, cut off from competition with their more efficient placental cousins, developing like forms for like environmental niches. So remote Tasmania can have its own 'tiger', which is not a tiger at all but something very different. The thylacine's uniqueness: it is a species, collectively discrete, indivisible, a genetic entity that can only produce its own kind, subject at some fork in the evolutionary tree to what Darwin describes as a 'distinct act of creation'.

Instead of comparing animals to men, she should be asking how they differ. And one answer when she thinks of men rather than man is obvious: animals are always honest. If you know the animal, you can always trust it, rely on it.

With animals there is no deceit, and that is one thing she has desperately sought and valued in her own life. Animals are always frank with their affections and desires and antipathies, and indeed, all her life Evelyn has recognised that these passions can be even as strong as her own.

For she considers it arrogance to assume that simply because animals, or so we suppose, largely lack conceptual thinking, and certainly language, they therefore feel, emote, any the less than man. On the contrary, because beasts have diminished capacities to rationalise the way man does, that probably means they are more often at the mercy of their instincts. And often, too often, it seems to her that her own complicated reasoning leads her away from what she really feels, and what she really needs.

Open and honest companionship. It is such a joy for her to contemplate the tiger waiting outside her hut in the morning. Simply because it wants to see her. She does not feed it; she has decided at the outset of their friendship against doing so, for ecological and also practical reasons. After all, she has only a certain supply of food for herself. Nevertheless, since she knows the thylacine to be mostly nocturnal, it must be breaking or at least seriously modifying its general habits to include her in its life. Then again, she did first sight it, and also made contact with it in open daylight. Still, animals are naturally conservative. So surely she can safely interpret this unsought fellowship as a genuine compliment.

Day by day out in the field, she loves the tiger's silent companionship, the unspoken but completely understood mutual sense of trust, the type of trust she has always hoped to achieve with a man but has never, and perhaps can never. She thinks it through again and again but always it comes down to this: the tiger can have no possible motive to be with her other than its affection for her, and could conceive of no reason for her to be with it but that same affection.

The cocoa has gone to her bladder. Again, she must break her train of thought, but when she returns to her bag, seemingly cold and awake, it is as though the reverie has been patiently waiting for her, so easily she slips back into it again…

Animals' greatest appeal for her is their independence, their sense of apartness. All beasts she has observed possess a natural unselfconsciousness; that is what will forever make them so particularly appealing and fascinating to self-conscious man, well beyond the old instinctual tie.

But if she is hyperconscious, the root of it is that she doubts, constantly. She can confess this to herself here in the dark. Constant doubting is also, as far as she can see, the underlying cause of any dependence she feels in her personal life. How she hates it, as she hates being dependent in any way.

It is an ingrained fantasy of hers to strip away all the trappings of civilised existence and step back into the wilderness, naked and pure. To range unfettered like her tiger through all this physical glory now radiating out from her, and also enclosing her in this shell-hut under the vast velvety night sky. To be a simple and natural part of it, some place, some way she can become like Adam before Eve, proud and alone, dwelling in mute harmony with the beasts.

Animals have such self-esteem, she thinks, a marked inbuilt sense of their own nobility, their own role and its importance. What is her role? In this hut, in this night?

Still, she must keep reminding herself, here she has a different role, which is in its way almost as important as the other, or even as her being the other, and that is to value and preserve it all. Because this is Eden, the tiger is here, and here it must stay and thrive. Which is ultimately her responsibility since she has found and befriended it. Now the tiger trusts her, she cannot fail it, for in this tiny oasis is probably its only chance of survival.

This little wilderness, like all wildernesses now, is an ark amidst the all-encompassing sterile salt sea of civilisation. Here still is one of Nature's wells, and for the tiger perhaps the last of them, as it is perhaps the last tiger, so here for the tiger is the final, the only regenerating source of life, the ur-womb. Thus beasts such as the tiger, coming from and living in such secret precious sources, become talismans, icons, archetypes of creation. And this is neither empty grandiosity, nor simple sentimentalism.

For she hates people sentimentalising animals, conversing with them about work or the weather, or putting baby words into their mouths as though they were substitute children. Humanising, diminishing them.

The tiger is emphatically not man, and loses nothing by it; on the contrary. She loves its silent dignity, although sometimes to her surprise she finds herself envious of it. It is so fit and right that the tiger cannot speak to her, nor possesses any other way to enmesh itself in a web of inane rationalisations. For it lives in a world apart, the wilderness, superior to man's world.

Finally, in the wilderness, in the tiger, no matter how much data she might accumulate, or how many conclusions she might formulate, there is something that will always be inaccessible to her. Maybe this is its greatest attraction, its final strength. Because it has a knowledge she cannot attain; it has a power she can never wield or subdue.

And all these general features of animals she has loved and contemplated for so many years are heightened, even epitomised in the thylacine, which is a grand solitary beast, a large carnivore at the head of the food chain, absolute lord of its mountain domain. So unique and rare, she sees it again standing at the top of Mount Jerusalem, looking out over a world of magnificence, single and proud, unchallengeable.

She considers once again rising and mixing some relaxant, but on the other hand, she is now both physically comfortable and at an extremity with her wakefulness, a state of heightened exhaustion, which she welcomes, because it probably means she will finally fall asleep for a few dawn hours. Now among the stream of conscious thoughts, vivid images on the verge of dreams come to her unbidden. She walks with her tiger through lush valleys and over cold high mountains, feeling something of it within herself, a positive exhilarating wildness.

These days that have been granted to her in the wilderness of the Walls of Jerusalem are imperishable. It occurs to her how her relationship with the tiger is in a peculiar way perfect. There is real friendship and mutual respect, without the messy insoluble complications of sex. And the beast doesn't challenge her at all in her own life, as even another woman might. There is a tacit acceptance that each has their own separate lives to lead and that these have an independent and unquestioned value.

Here is the very thing she has been seeking. Here is a relationship, that by its particular nature, that between man and beast, can never contain the seeds of possession, imbalance and destruction that, she increasingly believes, are destined to blight any relationship with her own kind, particularly the opposite sex. Here, somehow, she has found the balance without the stress.

Of course, she knows how wary she is of human personal commitment, particularly after Graeme, wary of being hurt again. She always over commits herself with men, with everything, and so this commitment, any commitment, has always proved traumatic and damaging. She is apparently simply avoiding all this with the tiger, having her cake and eating it too in a way, companionship and affection and perfect freedom without any personal threat.

And just for the present, even the very climate of the physical environment seems in balance, in harmony with all that is happening to her and all she is feeling. The inclement weather generally arriving by this time of year in the Central Highlands is holding off. The days are cold but mostly still and fine, excellent for her work, marvellous, bright and crisp. Although in a way there seems to be an artificiality about them in that they can be swept away at any moment. Each new sunny day links to its predecessor with a kind of nervous splendour. Their vulnerability, flukiness, increases their value, and binds them together in her mind like some fragile golden chain. Each morning opens out before her with seemingly limitless possibilities. Each morning she enters the wild as if borne on a great tide, reserving for the present the knowledge that any tide, in due course, must eventually ebb. For of course winter, savage and reckless, true regent of the highlands, is poised over this temporary stability of air and sky like a Damocles sword.

So she experiences the days with a sort of happy desperation, an inflamed expectation, like a person terminally ill, yet for the present trusting in the next sunrise. Her fieldwork has been recharged with significance and urgency; it is wonderful to feel so useful and good.

Lying there this long night, drinking in its quiet immensity, she knows another peerless morn will soon be upon her. The potent image of that ensuing golden light seeps through her like an elixir.

Finally, sleep is enclosing her like the gentlest of snowfalls. If only it were possible for her never to leave the wilderness, never to tell anyone and remain here with the tiger in this beautiful world, and make its world all her own.

While she can she will live only in the present, and dream of the lovely days still left her, and her fortuitously found perfect mateship, perfect world and perfect life.

Unravelling

'Do you ever, you know, write around your notes?'

'What do you mean?'

'Well, try to write some justification for what you're doing, why you're where you are.'

'I guess if I didn't know that, I'd be somewhere else.' Joseph doesn't want to sound flippant; he can hear she is serous. He wonders what kind of answer or response she wants to these elliptical questions? Why has she contacted him? 'Do you mean a précis, something like that? I thought I'd leave my introduction to the end, until I see what I've got all up, and what I can make of it in general terms.'

'That's not what I mean.'

'Right.'

'What I mean is that, as I write, I feel the need to question, and also to articulate as clearly as I can the subtext of my project. Of course this stuff won't appear in the report, except I guess by implication.'

'Sounds to me like time's a bit heavy on your hands.'

'Well, not really. Maybe…'

'The weather's been fine, plenty of good fieldwork opportunity.'

'The weather's been fabulous!'

Her exclamation comes out of Joseph's speaker with such a gust of passion that the voice distorts and he involuntarily shifts back on his oil drum.

'Well, since you were kind enough to pay me a visit, and the weather's holding, maybe I should reciprocate.'

'No! I mean, if it's okay, I'd just prefer to be on my own for the present. Although I might come and visit you again.'

'It'd be great to see you.'

'There's just something up here I need to sort out by myself.'

'Well, if you need a hand with anything…'

'Of course. Thanks. It's been good talking to you, Joseph. Yes, I'll definitely come over and see you.'

'I could use the company. Bit of contact's always good for the soul.'

'But don't call me, okay? I'll be in touch.'

'Look forward to it.'

'Speak to you shortly. Goodbye.'

'Goodbye, Evelyn.' He stares at the radio in his hand as though trying to divine its depths. Is she really all right?

Joseph, as it happens, does enjoy spending long stretches alone in the bush, although perhaps not this long, but he knows that this is pretty unusual, even for a bushie. Evelyn is strong and independent-minded, but presumably she has never experienced an extended period of enforced solitude like this. Still, she can contact him or the professor. She can walk over here, or drive back to Devonport, or even Hobart. She said she'd call on him soon, so he will wait on that.

His tone was sympathetic. She thinks it was a mistake to get in touch, perhaps like last time. Despite his intelligence, Joseph is a doer, not a thinker. Lucky him.

Evelyn glances at her watch. Two a.m. It was only nine when she rang off from Joseph. She must get herself ready for bed, but her mind is still buzzing. Perhaps simply going through bedtime routine, tidying up, changing, cleaning teeth will help calm her down. She reads again what she has just written: 'In some ways the world is fitted to us; in others it is clearly inimical. To strive is fundamental, not to arrive a condition of life. Stress here is the amniotic fluid, and highly motivated individuals, those who finish the second lap while the rest are struggling with the first, seem only fully content when operating under strain. And just as nature abhors a vacuum, if placed where there is little pressure, they will create it to establish their particular equilibrium.'

She is like one of the old pines, needing stress to achieve her natural shape. She knows this about herself, and she knows it has an adjunct: the greater the stress, the greater her need to believe it comes from outside, particularly when that is not the case. She has been caught out many times with this reflex, which, although it has value, can occasionally blind her.

In this she is like an athlete with an injury, who because they cannot feel pain in action, inadvertently injure themselves further through achieving further. Even her tendency towards doubt she finds herself increasingly believing, as doubt itself increases, to be something pushed upon her, again, even when she knows it is not.

All this has happened to her before, but what she can't understand is why it is happening here, now, in her perfect world, and to such an extent. Maybe writing about it will help, maybe not, but she must try something; at least it is a kind of handle.

Trying to discuss it with Joseph was a silly idea. How could she describe to him, for example, how in her perfect world, in a series of eerily disturbing déjà vus, certain 'things' she normally doesn't worry about are slowly building as sources of tension. Such as, whether or not she is eating enough, or the right variety of food, or getting sufficient sleep, even though she feels physically fine.

Item: she has never been a good sleeper and is used to ignoring it and working on. But recently she has been formulating a fixed idea as to how many hours she should be sleeping, and when it doesn't happen, it nags her that she might not be working at her optimum. There is no catch-up the following night to compensate. By her general calculations, she is not keeping pace, so then she must be falling behind, becoming gradually exhausted and not fully aware of it, perhaps because of that self-defence reflex. Her work must be suffering in places, and she should recognise it. But she cannot see where it is suffering, if it really is.

Item: as a matter of habit, she uses block-out on her face and hands, and now it is almost winter, but even so she is concerned that the few months spent out in the open might have done some damage to her skin. She shows a healthy tan, and thanks to one Italian grandparent on her father's side takes the sun well. But maybe for that very reason she has been complacent and blight has occurred of which she is unaware, just as she has read that most skin cancers are caused in childhood but do not show until middle age. And the depletion of ozone in the atmosphere, the gas that screens harmful ultraviolet rays, the 'hole' that has recently formed over Antarctica, has it spread as far north as Tasmania?

Item: she has come into contact with a large exotic mammal believed extinct; so at the other end of the biological scale she might equally come into contact with an infectious microscopic virus previously unknown or undiagnosed, and being ignorant of symptoms, not realise in time, and lie wasting in the cabin unable even to reach her shortwave radio. Recently in the United States, a zoologist working alone with prairie dogs died from, of all things, bubonic plague. No one, including him, knew what it was. Or she might break a leg, or anything really. In so many ways, it's dangerous being out here alone so far from anywhere.

Now she is continually fantasising about dying. It is not just the unknown virus; with cinematic vividness, she sees herself tumbling off cliffs, lost in snowstorms, bitten by tiger snakes, and so on. But she has reasoned it through, again and again: she is happiest alone. Anyway, she is not alone; there is the tiger.

She closes her notebook to stop herself writing any more, stop herself getting overwrought, although it is a little late for that. She is alone. Anything could happen. Of course she wanted to conduct this study on her own, would have made it a condition of acceptance if necessary. Joseph is also alone, as are the others.

It is now three a.m. She must be tired, and knows she must stop this endless unproductive thinking. Instead, she opens her notebook and reads again the passages she has just written.

Three big fat folders lie before her. How on earth did she ever write so much? The truth is that for months now she has been working away without really thinking about what she is doing. Possible problems concerning her work keep propagating of their own accord, like that undiscovered virus. She just can't help herself, and maybe that is the virus, has always been. For no good reason at all, and not even for any reason she can invent, day by day she feels her research material is getting out of control, even if it really is not, and she must still allow herself that positive possibility.

Evelyn remembers how buoyant she was when she left Professor Atherton in Hobart. She seemed to have a clear idea of her research priorities, and confidence in how she would order and organise her observations. She knows that when researching she does tend to be obsessive and gather too much material. But she felt that afterwards, particularly with the professor's guidance, she would be able to sort through things satisfactorily. And the difficult practical stuff, the trapping and tagging and tracking of the pademelons, has gone very well. Surely it is better to have too much than not enough.

But still, look at those folders! Somewhere, somehow, she must have lost sight of her original guidelines. So maybe everything she is doing now, maybe everything she has been doing the whole time is simply a compilation of ephemera, masses of data of little value. A wonderful, even unique opportunity to do substantial work has been spoilt. If this is the case, and at least she must also consider it possible, then it will completely negate her nascent academic career and the excellent degree she worked so hard, suffered so much, sacrificed so much to attain.

This business of the future is leading her back to the problem of the tiger. She has told herself she will not think of the tiger this evening.

Four a.m. She stands. Her legs are stiff and her head reels. Her temples are throbbing although she hasn't noticed until now. It will be day in a couple of hours. She should take some pills and lie down, tie something around her eyes to stop the light from keeping her awake.

She shuffles around aimlessly, bumping into things, taking twice as long as normal to perform habitual actions. A slip with her toothbrush cuts her upper gum; there will be an ulcer later. When she is finally in her sleeping bag, she forces herself to empty her mind. This takes great effort until the pills work. Then she relaxes and at last, thankfully, feels herself falling away.

As the days pass, Evelyn employs every mental trick she knows to combat this sense of her life becoming increasingly difficult to manage. She thinks back to key moments of intense stress in former times, some involving relationships, some not, when she would blow things wildly out of proportion, how first she lost perspective, and then, slowly, any capacity to judge. Minor problems suddenly became enormously important, indistinguishable from what really was important. Everything eventually mattered, every single thing, and even though in periods of lucidity and calm she knew that wasn't the case, she could never stave off a feeling of being overwhelmed by an immense futility and purposelessness.

In each of those situations, she recalls every step away from normality, and what kind of mess she would be in at the end. And here it is starting up again for some reason, and even the knowing it can't seem to prevent it. She has struggled so hard for self-knowledge. What she thinks she has learnt.

As she loses belief in her work, in herself, it becomes more of an effort to propel herself out of the hut and into the bleak cold air, to embrace purpose. But now with the traps long since stacked up outside, and plenty of material written up, she wonders if there anything much more for her to do. The only other real business she can think of is the trip across the tarn country to examine the ecology of the small virgin peak she selected for a general comparison.

Perhaps that is the core of the problem: there is not much to do. In a similar way to her finding herself creating stresses in what she has defined as a stress-free environment, Evelyn inadvertently begins to create practical problems where none previously existed.

Her little fuel stove has somehow developed a blockage in the synthetic hose running from the interchangeable gas cylinder to the tank of the stove, or maybe it is the valve that is faulty. Virtually the whole time she has been in the wilderness, she has cooked in the hut over the stone fireplace using wood as fuel. But it bugs her that the thing doesn't work. It is brand-new and was pushed upon her by an overenthusiastic employee of the hiking store she outfitted herself in Sydney before the trip. She spends more and more time fiddling with it to no real effect, except to anger herself, and what was originally meant to serve the purpose of a convenience and a labour-saving device actually becomes the opposite, a waste of time and a source of needless frustration.

To counteract what she fears might be a growing and perhaps irrational personal instability, she decides to establish detailed specific routines, such as setting an exact time for going to bed at night, whether she is tired or not, a thing she has never done before. What she eats for each meal, how much, how long she spends in the field, how many pages of notes she should take each day to guard against overwriting and force herself to be selective, the ideal proportion of time spent collating compared with collecting and observing, and so on.

Alongside this ritualising, to counteract her other problem of increasing disbelief in herself, and her work, is an endless conscious and unconscious stream of self-justification in all of her activities. Self-analysis, always a predominant feature of her thinking, now over-takes that thinking, augmenting a growing sense of inertia. She must stop and thoroughly examine absolutely everything, which in turns feeds a pervasive nihilism which, like a corroding acid, imperceptibly seeps into every cranny of activity and thought.

With her difficulty in sleeping, she suffers more of that type of nervous energy she hates so much, the wasted vitality that cannot achieve productively. Also, odd inexplicable bouts of tension seem to be on the rise. Suddenly, for no reason, out of nowhere, she is incredibly screamingly tense, then it just as mysteriously subsides.

At night, the wind is troubling her, as when she first arrived. And each day she can sense her old enemy, the headaches, ready to pounce.

Although, like the bad weather, they just hold off, presumably waiting their moment of greatest opportunity. She worries at these things, but worry only makes it all worse, and she knows it, and worries at it too.

Despite the weather still being uncertainly poised, Evelyn can clearly observe increasing conflict between the great natural forces surrounding her, even from local capricious changes within her own circle of activity. The sudden wild sweep of powdered snow across the high face of crags lit with the pale gold of a steadily fading sun; the ice like strange pavings of thin flat plastic gradually encroaching over still surfaces of deep mountain lakes; the small tarns now hard silver mirrors; the groves of dark green pine flecked with snow like a European Christmas fantasy; the enormous and freezing mists billowing from valley to valley, absorbing all sound, filling the lowlands with bitter wet and a damp cold, or when the wind is up, flowing in huge swaths of white void, alternately blotting out and making visible in entirely unpredictable sequences, different depths and facets of the surrounds; the icy wet boggy ground, the endless mud and muck, the bleak cries of the fat black crows, and always, slowly swelling, like some enormous pulse in the night, the profound but hollow terrifyingly huge sound of the wind, the wind like some scouring and scourging spirit over a land whose time has come, one of the wild horsemen of the Apocalypse. All these things invest land and sky with a savagery and grandeur, and on a scale of immensity she has never known, nor even imagined.

From the window of her cabin, she watches giant storms form, build and sweep across from the distant ranges of the south-west. They appear to approach with a slow and measured pace, but always arrive before she expects them, and with a fury that always takes her by surprise. More than once, she is caught almost too far from the hut, and a virtual life-and-death struggle is suddenly upon her for the few minutes left to reach the door. She learns to read the danger signs, but each time the storms strike more quickly and ferociously.

She is nothing in all this; it is too vast for her to deal with in any way.

Something in the wilderness, her Eden, now seems totally out of control, which terrifies yet excites her. She witnesses it repeatedly, but cannot understand how the face of nature can change so swiftly and completely from benign majesty and solemnity to such wild savage malevolence, although this malevolence also has its own strange majesty.

Now the tiger only appears in the decreasing spells of fine weather. At other times, particularly during the snowstorms, Evelyn would willingly welcome it into the hut. But with the exception of that one day when it savaged her pack, it has shown no interest in her private domain, her den. Since they have subsequently established such a close relationship, this piques her.

Continually she frets over the tiger, both its friendship with her, and the problem of its future, which she first ignored, then postponed. But with her project completion date approaching inexorably like one of those storms, the impossible conundrum weighs upon her more heavily with each personal contact.

In Bob Baines's notes, thylacines almost always keep in family groups, so the tiger being a loner and becoming attached to her probably means it is the last of its kind in this area. This uniqueness coupled with the unusual friendship initially gave her great pleasure, which continues, but is now alloyed by a theoretical zoological regret over there being no breeding population. This would be the optimum situation, sufficient tigers to ensure the species' continuance. Therefore, as a dedicated zoologist, how can she rejoice in the beast's solitariness, particularly in relation to herself, with a clean conscience?

She simply cannot imagine her thylacine taken from its magnificent kingdom and placed in a zoo or reserve. That is impossible. General policy of Parks and Wildlife when faced with the situation of a rare and threatened species, or one previously thought extinct being discovered, is to close off the general area, try and isolate the animal or plant, give it a chance. But that seems impossible here. The Walls of Jerusalem is not some obscure valley surrounded by others. It is a famously spectacular scenic area, increasingly popular.

Somehow the news would get out. Then people would come, the media. It would take only one crazy with a gun. And already she has aided and abetted this by befriending the tiger. She could just not inform the authorities, the professor, anyone, but the end result would still be the same. The tiger exists, and sooner or later someone else will see it and photograph it. Much as she would like to, she cannot simply walk away. Her silence, or inaction, will mean the creature's death.

She could falsify some of her research material so that the hiker degradation seems far worse than it is, and the park might be closed a while longer to give her a little breathing space, try and work out some other solution, but that goes hard against the grain. Evelyn holds high ideals of honesty in scholarship, and within herself. She feels she is actually incapable of writing a convincing report she doesn't believe in, and Professor Atherton will be overseeing the material.

No doubt the animal will fret when she leaves. She cannot bear to think of it wandering the mountains and valleys, pining for her and searching in vain. She knows how dogs and cats sometimes worry themselves to death when their masters die or abandon them.

Now she has ambivalent and confused thoughts about the animal that have arisen silently alongside her doubts over her work. When she regards the self-possession of the tiger, for her its greatest fascination, an odd animosity mingles with her love. When it looks at her directly with those strange eyes, wilderness eyes, it feels to her like a challenge. She cannot avoid seeing this response in herself for what it is, a peculiar type of jealousy.

Conversely, the docility of the beast now irritates her for the opposite reason. How could she have tamed such a wild and special animal, and so easily? How has it become so dependent upon her? It is a kind of servility, and any servility reduces a creature's natural dignity. Thinking about this, more than anything else, triggers pain in her head. Because if the best kind of relationship she can possibly conceive of is also somehow tainted, what is the point of any relationship, or anything at all?

Another World

The writing is finished. She can do no more, and as far as she can see there is no need. She has enough, more than enough. If the editing, the sorting, is beyond her at present, it can wait.

One nominally set task remains: the trek across tarn country to the small isolated peak. It is not a necessary business and maybe she won't write it up, but it might prove interesting, and it also might help give her work, and herself, some needed perspective. At the very least it will give her something to do. Her allocated time here is not yet complete, and she must do something, otherwise she will just sit around brooding endlessly over the tiger. She is not sleeping these nights, so an early start is no problem.

One morning, kitted up, Evelyn steps out purposely into the burning cold. The tiger is nowhere to be seen. She is relieved; she does not want the complicated pressure of it with her today. The sun must have risen but is not visible; there is only a dim general light through an even veil of cloud. The muddy ruts her boot-prints have made outside the door of the hut are now iced hard and sharp, difficult to traverse.

Buoyed to be moving, doing, she crunches through the silver grass, smashing the thick glass of the puddles like a child. Occasionally she disturbs a wallaby or bird. The snakes would all be sleeping, curled tight in their burrows. The brooks have sunk into silence. Occasionally she hears the faint sharp retort of a distant branch as it cracks in the freezing air. The cloud veil thins and the sky becomes a mirror, the sun a pale disk. The only birds abroad seem to be the crows, ark, ark, ark; in the bleak landscape, their harsh cawing conveys a sense of desolation beyond expression. She actually comes across one dead and stiff on the ground, all the lustre leached from its feathers, that blue-black beauty. She is surprised at its sheer size and wonders how such a successful scavenger could just die.

After a few hours, Evelyn reaches the tarns and progresses cautiously, ensuring, as she painstakingly edges around the large angled waters through sloshy icy loam, that she maintains her direction. She is toiling haphazardly along an extensive shallow declivity and the peak is presently hidden from her.

Suddenly, she sights it again; it is considerably larger than expected, and much further away. The map here must be inaccurate. Maybe she will need to camp on it. It looms up forbidding, pure and glacial, the broad summit capped by a great slab of glistening white. She will continue for an hour, and then make a decision.

As she approaches the peak across an immense high plain, the ground dries and hardens, the air brightens and she is slowly overtaken by a strange phenomenon. The entire landscape appears to be breaking up, separating out into its component parts. It is becoming trees and ground and water, and making no sense to her as a whole, an entity.

She comes to a halt. She doesn't know what has happened here, but all at once she does know she can progress no further, no closer. The peak is firmly before her, clear and upright, but it is as if a magic circle has been drawn around it, a force field she cannot penetrate.

She remembers how one of her university course lecturers, a Chinese national, once told her class how lead hunters in his native village traditionally employed ancient incantations which they used to partly control natural forces, specifically to drive wild animals into pits and snares. She was fascinated by this and quizzed him further. He told her those more steeped in this lore believed they could erect 'demon walls', powerful spells on the landscape that prevented travellers from moving forward, or forced them to walk in large circles unknowingly. It is something like this that Evelyn has come up against here, but it is nature casting the spell, not man.

Maybe she needs the tiger, her natural 'guide', if she wishes to enter this field, break through the 'wall', to act as her interpreter. Or maybe for some reason she is not yet ready, not fully prepared, initiated, her coming here is premature. But for whatever reason, it is a plain fact that she cannot proceed. This peak will remain for her an unattainable, inviolate sanctuary. After this attempt she will not try again, and she implicitly understands that she must accept this strange exclusion and not question it.

Complete silence descends and takes hold. The landscape all around becomes more abstract, line and form. Loss of place, of location, a fundamental fear from childhood. She cannot make sense of this world, without the tiger's help, without her translator.

She could become nothing, simply lie down on this iron ground and be washed clean by the successive seasons, a *tabula rasa*. It is better to admit she was innocently wrong in coming here and return before the landscape becomes so strange that she cannot find her way back. She takes a last look at the peak, and turns around. She could not move forward, but to her considerable relief retracing her ground is not difficult, the landscape gradually recomposes itself.

But maybe her tiger, her titular spirit, has been with her after all, for as she approaches the hut the temperature plummets sharply, the air becomes tense and electric, and with little warning a snowstorm strikes with jagged fury. She has time to make the hut, but would definitely have been caught out had she continued any closer to the strange mountain. Providence and the tiger.

Throughout the remainder of that bitter day, a sequence of storms descends on the Walls with increasing savagery, and by nightfall it seems that Evelyn will be trapped in the hut once again with her unquiet meditations.

Recently she has been suffering from a continuous low-grade headache, which has periodically flared up into real pain, then subsided with the help of medication. With this, she has felt both exhausted and also brimming with nervous energy. Although she is not sleeping, at night she makes herself lie down for the requisite hours; she closes her eyes and tries to empty her mind, think of nothing. But she knows this sustained wakefulness, from past experience, generally bodes ill. She is living on her reserves. The day after her trek to the peak, as the weather rages outside, Evelyn paces fitfully around the cold little square of the hut, like an animal in a cage, searching in vain for any useful tasks she might perform.

She also paces around to try and walk away from her sore head. She has not been too concerned about the headaches until this confinement. She is pretty used to them and there have been other more significant things for her to worry about. But with the settling in of this storm, there also settles a thicker more pervasive pain, perhaps linked to atmospheric pressure. Not only does the pain itself increase, it changes in quality, seeming substantial, even permanent. The analgesics she is now regularly ingesting, the strongest possible for her condition, seem only to dehydrate and nauseate her, and in the long term are bad for her kidneys.

As she paces the room, this way and that, hour after hour, Evelyn starts to formulate the notion that her headaches are somehow connected with the ceaseless howling wind, which, now she considers it, has troubled her from the outset. Of course she has suffered sequential headaches like this before. Nevertheless, she cannot prevent herself believing that on this occasion, the unearthly hollow whining has been driving the pain into her head like a nail, thud, thud, thud, and unless she can find a way to block its influence, it might drive her mad. She tries plugging her ears with cotton wool from her medical kit and this alleviates the pain to a degree, giving further credence to her theory.

With nothing else she can see to do of any practical use, she fiddles intermittently but persistently with the fuel stove, and on the second day of the storm, in a sudden fit of frustration, breaks it irreparably. This depresses her so deeply she sits with the pieces in her open hands, with tears of rage flowing, for a full hour. The slight but possible danger of her being caught between hut and car with no means to cook doesn't vex her nearly as much as the futility of all her efforts with the stupid appliance.

What else? There is her camera, her Olympus Trip with a thirty-six-shot roll inside, thirty-three used, twenty-five or so of the thylacine. She has another new thirty-six-shot roll. She should rewind the almost finished roll and secure it and install the new roll for further possible multiple shots. When she is out on the trail, she carries her camera as a matter of course. Although she keeps it wrapped in a plastic bag, it is still possible it could become wet, or slip out of her hands and smash in a fall.

But incredibly – she cannot believe this dwelling on it afterwards – Evelyn unthinkingly opens the back of the camera before she has rewound the film, thus exposing the roll. She immediately snaps it shut and rewinds the film but what damage has she done? She cannot know. She will be able to take more shots when the weather clears again; presumably her companion will still be around. Probably all is all right, but just possibly it is a disaster. This plunges her back into a depression, although for some reason not as severe as that with the stove. What will she wreck next? In her present state, she must leave all mechanical appliances alone.

There are her notes; she cannot break those. She could make one last heroic effort to sort them out. Once again, Evelyn applies herself to the reorganisation of her research material, but as she has really known in advance, the more she looks at all she has written, invariably, inevitably, the more befuddled she becomes.

She spreads out the pages onto the cold dusty flagstones and crouches there staring blankly at them for hours. Then she tears herself away, tries to divert herself with some absurd non-task, checking her supplies, polishing her boots, clear the muddle in her mind a little. She returns to them, occasionally swapping the order around, touching them meaninglessly, obsessively, worrying them like an animal might a wound, and slowly a sort of existential feeling comes over her whereby the very words that she herself has written, some only last week, lose all syntactical and individual meaning, and become weird and absurd hieroglyphs, completely indecipherable.

She worries that some of her domestic routines are beginning to break down (did she brush her teeth this morning?), while conversely others are becoming more detailed and fanatic (why must she keep checking her supplies?). She is so concerned to do this thing how it must be done that she forgets about doing that other thing, which, when she thinks about it, is more important, or is it?

All of this is silly; she doesn't really have to do anything. She can just stay in bed and shelter from the cold for the period of the white-out, reading or dozing. But she just cannot stand the thought that time is passing, and she is doing nothing substantial. Which means she is going backwards. For some reason, for no reason, a weight of urgency increasingly presses down on her, but serving only to further immobilise her.

Eventually, she ends up in front of the cold ashes of the fireplace stirring the dust idly with a stick, trying through the pain in her head and the ever-present sound of the wind to work out what on earth she is going to do with herself and the tiger. Her tiger. That is the only real problem, the one she has been trying to avoid, the one impossible to avoid, impossible to solve, the problem behind all other problems.

She reruns the arguments. What if she stays here? With her tiger. Is that possible? They will come in, eventually. They will have to. They will come in and find her. Let's say they do come in and find her. What will they say to her? What will they do? And the tiger, her special friend, this unique relationship, how can she explain it to them? How banal, sentimental, how utterly ridiculous it will all sound in their ears. How can they possibly understand?

They will ask her questions that she cannot satisfactorily answer. Why did she delay radio contact? What has she been trying to prove? Is she aware how much worry and cost she has caused? And the tiger.

It is a huge zoological discovery, an historical discovery of international significance. Why didn't she report it immediately? What is she really trying to do here?

They will accuse her of hiding her discovery. This deceit on her part, for such a length of time, will make them naturally disbelieve anything else she tells them. They will think she is lying to them about everything, so then they will think she has been lying to them all along. She knew about the tiger even before she went to Hobart. She saw it plainly on her initial trip in and she knew then that it was no dog. She is a zoologist. How could she seriously expect anyone to believe that someone with her training, and also her grades, could possibly mistake a thylacine for a dog?

Maybe they know that anyway. It's a possibility; she has to consider it. Maybe they know all about the tiger, have known about it all along. With all those previous sightings, how could they not know, or at least strongly suspect? If they know about the tiger, then it follows they must know about her. Then why have they let her go on and on like this? Maybe they are testing her in some way. Whatever it is, she has failed. God knows she has failed miserably, and now they know that too. And soon they will be coming in, for her and for her tiger.

Maybe they are coming in right now. How her head rings! Surely they will not enter the park in this weather. Unless they are really well equipped and determined. What can she do? She is helpless in the grip of this relentless storm and her state of mind and health. They will come in and they will wreck everything. She must stop them. Evelyn is suddenly seized by the need for intense committed action, but cannot even begin to imagine what kind of action she should take.

Perhaps she can go away with her tiger. Go away with her special friend. But where? How could she live? A big gong starts striking deep in her head. How can she do anything with all that noise? Stop it! Please just stop it!

Her rush of thought is arrested by an awareness of a sharp high sound above the storm, the raised sound of her own voice. With a shock she realises that she has been talking out loud, talking to herself. Shouting even.

She sits mum, and hugs her knees tightly to stop herself shaking. Her words still hang in the air, a ghostly presence. Herself as a madwoman. She maintains this position, making herself think of nothing until her body stills. How long she been doing this, talking to herself? She must take her mind off the tiger. Perhaps look at her notes again. But with this thought, her pain intensifies wildly. She grips her head. She is not coping. What she can do? Always the same questions she cannot answer.

She searches around for a scarf and then binds it tightly around her head and ears. This, with the cotton wool, dulls the sound of the wind a bit more and again the pain decreases. One step forward after several backward. She sits and listens to the muffled storm. It rages without respite.

The tiger belongs to her. It knows that too. They cannot just come and take it from her. She thinks of their relationship being broken, of them taking the mute beast and her looking on helplessly and it not understanding, and a great spasm of grief shakes her, she bursts into tears, and then uncontrollable sobbing. So she must again squat on the floor and claw back control.

But where is the tiger? She recalls friends and lovers she trusted who eventually betrayed her. Is it possible the tiger is also struggling against her affection like those? That sense of apartness she found so attractive in the tiger. It has a life apart from hers. It lived quite happily before she arrived. Presumably, she thinks, it can live quite happily after she has gone.

This maddens her. Her pain increases. She tightens the scarf. She is not irrelevant. She is important to the tiger, perhaps the single most important element in its life. She knows that, and surely it knows that. She is missing it, thinking about it, worrying. It knows where she is, knows how to find her. It knows she will welcome it.

Evelyn tries to imagine where the tiger is. Concentrating, taking her time, she goes deep inside herself for the knowledge, tries not to rationalise, work out, but rather intuit where it might be, and what it might be doing. See through its eyes.

She focuses solely on feeling for the beast, and then there rises before her an extraordinarily detailed image of it sheltering near the base of a giant crag, foraging idly. With even greater effort and focus, she recognises the crag as Mount Jerusalem; she can now clearly see its familiar planes and folds in their magisterial splendour, highlighted by a light sprinkling of snow.

She has managed to locate the tiger precisely, and even over the tumult of the storm can distinctly hear it sniffing among the shrubbery, and most amazingly, the barely audible susurration of the padding and scraping of its paws. Even more focus and she is finally bonded, fused, with the creature's own instinctive life, the warmth of its body, the beat of its blood. Now she feels she knows the tiger in the same way as it must have known her pademelon, Henry, on that very first day.

But for her to be able to do this, she sees that the tiger must exist completely inside as well as outside of her. In a strange way, she has completely enclosed this wild beast.

The heightened pain from this forces her up on her feet to pace the room again. She has stopped crying, and her mind is now revolving furiously. So, what more can she make of this unique, extraordinary vision? Is the tiger trying to reach her? That is really what she needs to establish. It appears to be sheltering, but then what kind of sheltering is this, struggling along the base of Mount Jerusalem? Why isn't it holed up somewhere, somewhere sensible, instead of obviously risking death, or even perhaps dying trying to reach her.

Evelyn focuses within again and another vivid picture of the beautiful dying beast, prostrate in a wild snowy wasteland racked with cold, exhaustion and want of her, flashes into her mind filling her with intense grief and a curious satisfaction. Emotion flows from her like blood from a wound. Cathartic tears well up. She reminds herself that this is the creature's natural environment. Snowstorms are frequent in the Walls of Jerusalem and it must be used to them, used to taking care of itself.

Unless, of course, she herself has disturbed this. Maybe its want to be with her is stronger than its natural will for survival. No, that is silly. It's a wild animal, instinct will always predominate. Think of the professor's muttonbirds traversing half the globe and returning to the same little burrow. Muttonbirds, Hobart, it seems such an age away. She must try and get a hold of herself. But it is so difficult with the wind and pain.

She sits down again in front of the cold fireplace, and tries to think the whole business through in a calm and considered manner. But it seems to her that either the tiger is out dying trying to reach her, or it doesn't care for her. She can't see any other alternative and both fill her with bleak despair and impotent anger.

Can she go out and look for it? She would be lost metres from the hut. But maybe the weather has partly abated. From where she is sitting, the opaque black of the small cabin window blocks her vision as if from malevolent design. She could venture out a little. Maybe it is out there trying to get in and she cannot hear it!

Evelyn races to the door, shifts the rock, and edges the frame slightly outwards. The wind catches it, almost tearing it from her hands. Big flakes of snow rush into the cabin. It is hopeless, she can do nothing. And it is dark now, night has closed in already, which is another thing she hasn't noticed. Only four o'clock and night. She brings her stiff hands up to her face and they are like ice, not part of her. It feels below zero; she must warm herself.

She returns to the fireplace and rouses it into activity. When the flame catches and settles, the heat and light cheer her so much she is surprised to contemplate how down she must have been.

The fire grows and crackles comfortably, thawing her hands and face. The warmth seems like sanity, although she notes, with a slight inward tremor, just how precisely the brightness of the flames registers the rise and fall of the constant wind. But it is relaxing, and her pain eases. Occasional snowflakes, forced by the gale through gaps in the shingles above, drift down, sparkling, then vanishing in the glow of the fire. All that business about them coming in for her. That was silly. She should organise some dinner, even though she has no appetite.

She heats a small tin of tomato soup but is unable to finish it. The headache and pills. This pain in her head, the noise of the wind. She sits staring into the fire watching the rest of the soup boil away, leaving a solid crusty black residue in the saucepan she will need to scour out.

The hours drag on and the fire gradually dies. She realises she is cold again. She gets into bed and listens to the wind and the beating in her head. The hours drag on immeasurably. She rises, takes more pills than she should, then returns to bed and falls into a strange spell of pain and wind. Again, she tries to empty her mind, think of empty things, a disused back-country road, arising out of nowhere, leading to nowhere, and above it, a huge sky with vast continental masses of clouds, so beautiful, slowly drifting, empty things, and then she does manage to float for a while, drift, like those clouds.

Evelyn is aware that the room has become lighter, and for some reason she feels she is entering a new world. The surrounding light grows so slowly she imagines it must be painful for this world to appear in its fullness, perhaps like birth. Everything is the colour of metal.

Finally, it is daylight. Grey light seeps through cracks in the hewn stone beside her face. She rises. She feels terrible. Her head now is as bad as she can ever remember; she is nauseous from the pain. There is no point in taking any more pills. She drinks a little water, but it tastes foul. She can't eat; there is no point in trying. She slumps in front of the dead embers of the fire, her head drooping in the grey cold light, the metallic light, and simply cannot move.

She thinks for a while about why she cannot move. Not that there is any point in moving, doing. No reasons left for her. Then, bizarrely, nothing happens at all, absolutely nothing. There is a stay in time's irreversible juggernaut, the world is unoccurring. She is her headache, and that is all. No, there is the wind, also with a timeless, non-time quality. The pain within, the wind without.

Then much later, at some stage, she realises the wind has died. Finally the storm has passed over. Silence has crept back to fill all available space. She listens to it, the silence, and it seems incredible, miraculous. Now it penetrates her, spreads completely within, to her fingertips, her toes. She listens more closely, noting how this pervasive silence naturally exaggerates other unassimilated sounds, such as the rustling of her clothes and the trickling of melting snow on the roof from what must be the sun. And the bird calls, painful jabs of sound, sharp as ice.

Evelyn looks at her watch, which she has completely forgotten about. Interprets the dial with difficulty. Half past three in the afternoon. The sun will set shortly. Her headache has receded a little but the pain is still strong, and seems even more deeply rooted. It has battened on her permanently, it will be with her for the rest of her life. She stands up and falls. Her left leg is completely numb through loss of circulation. She massages it and slowly through shooting sparks of pain, of life, the blood returns.

She pushes back the rock and throws open the door. A long quadrangle of pale light falls on her and the cold air sweeps over her, shocks her, and tightens the skin on her face so it feels like a mask. She closes her eyes in ecstasy. How beautiful, the cold air, fresh and pure and clean. She opens her eyes again. The sky is clear. A heavy blanket of deep white covers all the visible land, almost as deep as life itself, seemingly deeper, and here outside the silence is more powerful, a palpable and even ominous presence.

After staring at the snow a while, letting it dazzle, enter her, it becomes impossible for her to believe that any earth lies beneath. The shapes of the landforms are familiar, but they have been transformed, integrated into a vast uniform sculpture. That pungent distinctive snow smell. Yes, it is a new world. There is nothing now but the clear blue sky and the pure crushed crystal of snow stretching away on all sides.

The second recognition strikes her almost as quickly as the first. It is her old world transformed. The world glimpsed that first day from the plane, her perfect world, her paradigm. She has come to it at last. All at once her heart dilates with a frantic joy. Then she pauses in her exaltation and listens again to the silence, and lets the slow breathing of the wilderness become her own, help still the beating of her heart.

She re-enters the cabin and dons her snow gear, then walks back out into the huge brightness of her new world. Her boots squeak on its shining floor, the floor of heaven. She shivers from it, but also, inexplicably, from fear of herself. Stepping on your own grave, as they say. She stops. Now it all looks slightly different, still perfect, but something has happened. The light has shifted, subtly, even in the brief period she has been back in the hut.

So it seems each time she turns away and then looks at it again, this world will be perfect in a slightly different way, like the individual snow-flakes themselves, it will show her a subtly different pattern, a variable, different possibility of formal perfection. Time minutely shifts the cylinder of the kaleidoscope.

In reality, it is the paradox of a perfect continuum, always changing, always ideal, like some beautiful organism. While she watches it, the land is slowly drinking the light, draining it away. To see this, she needs to also slow herself right down, like she achieved that time long ago on the Maria Island ferry.

She stares hard at the sun as it leans towards the wild white horizon. It has lost all its warmth. It looks the same but something is wrong. Intense panic suddenly grips her. The solitude of the wilderness has finally entered her soul, but not to grant a philosophic calm; for some reason, it now provokes in her a frenzy. She must be unconsciously fighting against it. She closes her eyes and lets the cold air calm her again, and gradually, gradually she feels her heart beat more slowly. That's it. Let the cold still her heart, fix it like ice.

She steps beyond the shadow of the cabin to where the snow is new, soft, difficult to negotiate. Snow is so lovely and so deadly for the hiker. She knows there is some necessary link between its beauty and its deadliness, but in her exhaustion and exaltation she cannot see what that link is. But then of course she has now reached a state where intuition has complete precedence, mastery, over thought.

She shuffles down towards the creek. She recalls how, after a time, this was a route she knew so well that she could walk it with her eyes shut, feeling the sun on her face, and open them just at the edge of the little rocky pool she used as a basin. Now the creek is frozen but not covered, and where its line marks the naked landscape, it appears to her briefly like a black vein on the skinned carcass of the earth. She scrapes the snow from the surface of the pool.

Because the ice has continually fractured and re-formed, it lies packed in different shaded layers, showing patterns like little spider's webs where the drops have trickled down to a central weak point. The larger patterns of the same sort look like a network of human veins, or maybe the nerve patterns of the brain. When Evelyn shifts her focus slightly, she can see a distorted reflection of herself in the ice. Her image is thus twisted and strange; she cannot bear to look at it, although she finds it fascinating. She wrenches her eyes away and gazes up towards the horizon.

The sun is almost touching the earth. It has become orange, and larger. Still it has no heat, but it does have marginally more presence. The sun is dead, she knows, but here it is flaring up one last time, one slow beat, pulse, before expiring. It gradually turns red. This moment of final transition she can see clearly, but she knows that when she re-enters the hut, outside the small blank window it will be full night. The red rim dips behind the horizon, and the image, movement, strikes her as significant. Then it is gone. All that is left is a fading glow and a veil of spiritual pearliness in the sky.

She returns to the hut. Before she shuts the door, Evelyn turns for a final view. As the colours fade, she sees how much better it all is without the sun, how much finer. There is nothing alien now to disturb the symmetry of earth and sky. The creek is below her sightline and the limitless expanse of form is seamless, and while she watches, the limited palette of tone draws steadily towards a perfection of nullity.

Another End

Rather than obscuring the professor's voice, the crackle and whine accompanying it over Joseph's radio serve to highlight its tension and concern.

'She's missed two scheduled call-ins, she doesn't answer my calls, and I'm pretty certain she hasn't tried to contact me. I should get Search and Rescue onto it but before I do, because of the type of person she is, I would like you to go in first.'

'She won't like it.'

'You don't need to say I sent you. She visited you, you visit her. Well, what do you think?'

'I think something's wrong.'

'And report back immediately.'

'Okay.'

Something is wrong, Joseph knows it in his bones. He's never been one to move swiftly and confidently to a resolution. He has always liked to take his time, and sometimes this has told against him. If by some chance he has made a mistake, a woman with the pride of Evelyn Carter would never forgive him for his meddling. Perhaps even if he has not.

There is nothing really to go on but his intuition. Her visit was odd, but not in any way he could put his finger on at the time. The call too, and they both seemed more so in retrospect. It has long been a failing of his to understand things only well after they have occurred, but eventually, dwelling on it through the frosty nights, what has crystallised in Joseph's mind is some kind of cry for help. Help from

what he does not know, and perhaps it is unconscious, but a cry nevertheless.

But then, with the crucial trigger of the professor's call, impossible
weather descends, rain and sleet and more rain, full blizzard snow for
her up on the plateau no doubt. Just static on the shortwave. After days
of this, and seemingly at one stroke, the skies clear, and Joseph, his big
body bridling at the long containment, throws together an emergency
pack and fords the swollen stream to his car. Despite the canvas
waterproofing, it takes him half an hour to start the engine, but soon
enough he is careering along the lake road, sluicing through mud,
ducking around potholes, eyes peeled for the turn-off to the Walls. He
must hurry, for already in the rear-view mirror he can see another front
building.

Evelyn crouches on the top of Mount Jerusalem in the bitter pre-dawn
frost. She feels the circumambient air slowly crust over her like a
carapace, a second skin, claiming her. As similarly, spread out beneath
and before her, with its vast snowy mantle, the landscape she loves and
knows by heart has been miraculously superseded, claimed. There is a
voice in the back of her mind telling her she shouldn't be here, some
tiny hysterical woman's voice back of the huge calm, she can almost see
the figure in the far distance writhing alone on an empty plain. Just as
she thinks she actually sights it, it fades, loses focus, and dissolves back
into the billowing mist.

Is it perhaps because there is some other place she should be? She
doesn't even know how she got to be wherever she is. Has she crossed
the tarn wasteland? Or did she decide against that? The trouble is the
pain. But that is always the trouble. She cannot think, just be aware of
the pain. Her body is wholly numb from the cold. It is strange the cold
cannot numb her head-pain as well. No true sensation except that
pain. Time no longer matters; she has done with it.

The sun springs up in the icy wind like a fierce avenger, an armed
man. It burns before her with its fires of ice. The sky is so large,

terrifying and exhilarating in its clarity and purity. She is exposed to the face of God. Infinity is everywhere, the boundless world springs out from her, and yet also it is closing in, always closing. It flings out from her and compresses simultaneously, presses in on her head with its immense weight. Exhilaration and pressure unbearable, her, at the centre of the world, the world of pain.

She recalls a room-mate of hers, when she boarded for a few months at University College, who suffered from severe period cramps. Each month for days, this girl was crippled, locked in. Evelyn was fascinated by someone suffering such an abundance, a luxury of pain, and asked her to describe it. The girl shocked her by saying the only thing comparable to it was sex, because the pain and sex were the only things she knew that contained the same quality of abandonment. They blotted out everything, and became everything. You were helpless in it and yet you possessed an enormous power of experience. Pleasure, pain, the dividing line was not clear. What was clear was the abandonment, the shedding of the known world. And the power.

Now she is what that girl described. The old world has been sloughed off, a chrysalis, and here is this new world, agonising and ecstatic, charged with that immense experience. Great knowledge, vision, necessarily entails great pain. And power entails responsibility.

They will be here soon. They do not belong in this new world of hers. They are coming for her tiger, the last one in the perfect world. It is of this new world, her tiger, this perfect world, and will not be apart from it. She is the only one who can see this, who has striven and succeeded to this through her pain. She feels herself stretch out over the earth and air in throbbing agony. This world, her tiger, they cannot be shared, it is impossible. If they try, if they come in, her perfect world will necessarily shatter, like shards of ice.

The light is hard and sharp as a knife, and the wind rising. She can see the shape of the wind as it leans on the land. Fleet shadows from isolated clouds race across the snowscape like animate beings. The wind is rising, coming. The cold is only bearable because she knows her pain is greater. Now she sees: she shouldn't hate the wind, it is her ally in this new world. She has been wrong to resist it. It is right, even perfect that the wind blows so hard. She has hated the noise, but she sees now it is right that the real world, the perfect world, is hard and implacable in all of its facets, like a crystal.

For this is the world she saw from the plane, her paradigm, the pure white world. On that day, in the plane was an intimation of this world. She had known that. And then there was pain in her head, not sustained, but intense, another intimation. Her pain, this wilderness. The wind now blows into her with greater force, she feels the cold increasing its power, but her pain is more powerful. Clouds push up from the horizon, big passionate clouds, clouds upon clouds. A front. The weather is turning yet again.

Evelyn tries to rouse herself. She has never been this bad. She should get down and into the hut, but she just crouches there, unable to move with the pain and the beauty. So achingly lovely, the unpolluted world sprung from her throbbing brain. Clouds upon clouds, wild winter wind, she weeps for the beauty and the pain. The tears stream down her face and the wind fixes them on her cheeks. Crystals. But she is not sobbing, her body is rigid. She weeps for the pain and the power, and for the wonderment of it all.

Huge sulphur clouds surge in the sky with the distinct smell of snow. She should get down. How much time has passed? Time is of no account. What happened yesterday? She can't remember. Did she eat? She must eat, it is important. But it's so difficult to eat all the right things at the right time in the right amounts. It was another world. But she should make sure she eats properly. She must get down. Make a move. Soon it will be too late. The weather is breaking up. These thick clouds, now they cover her perfect sky. And clouds in her brain too. God, she must get down!

She crouches there, locked. Then, with an enormous application of will, she forces herself up. Her joints are stiff and she cannot straighten properly. Sharp lights pop and streak across her vision. She breaks into a run, stumbling madly down the steep rocky cliff through the snow, hardly knowing, thinking, the pain is so intense. Down in the valley, all around her are masses of new snow, glistening alabaster sheets of broad terraces, huge fantastic drifts and dunes sculpted by the wind, changing even as she watches them.

There is blood on her jeans. She has gashed her leg. She regards the blood quizzically, pokes the wound. She looks at the blood on her hands; it too is pure. She puts it to her lips and tastes its salt sweet. Then the wind knocks her down into the snow. She picks herself up, pushes on. She is now on the flat, ploughing through the powder snow against the wind, limping a little, mindful of possible wet holes as she crosses the stream.

There, at last, is the hut. Weird out of the wind. Her pain seems much worse out of the wind. What is it she came for? She knows if she stands here it will come to her. She cannot withstand the pain for long without moving and also out of the wind. She must hurry. What is it? Of course! Here it is! Soon they will be arriving. Yes, she must hurry.

She walks out into the wind and it throws her against the side of the hut, cutting right through her clothing and into her flesh. Snow-flakes are whirling in a mad devil-dance. She must hurry. She pushes on behind the hut into the forest of pencil pines. It is more sheltered, but the cold is still intense, deepening and strengthening. The wet black trunks crowd in on her, baleful and alien. The wind rises to a hollow scream. It is both outside the forest and inside her. It is almost a voice, another voice she recognises, like the pain in her head. The voice and the pain are the same. She has been so terrified of the wind and the pain but now they are inside her and the fear, it is still there she knows, but has become irrelevant, like that woman writhing on the distant plain.

The wind is the trumpets of Jerusalem blowing from the four corners of the perfect kingdom. Her head is bursting with the howling cold. She can feel her strength failing, the vision faltering, but she must hold on. She has the power and the responsibility, here, clenched right in her hand. Where is the place? She must find it, before her strength fails her. Yes, here it is, waiting for her.

She limps into the small clearing. High above the trees meet in an ogive, swaying in and out of focus with the howling wind, bending gracefully with her pain, rubbing and whispering conspiratorially. Here is her beauty. What weird eyes her beauty has, eyes of the wilderness. She caresses the soft ears and tears run down her face. What eyes, trusting but strange, eyes of the wilderness. They challenge her no longer. She kneels down and cradles the creature's head in her arms, gentles the loose soft flesh at its neck. She cries silently, deeply, stroking her love over and over.

There is nothing else she can do. They will never understand. Huge waves of pain pulse through her, an ocean of pain. She is drowning, her strength failing. She has seen it, that much has been vouchsafed, the crystal before it shatters. The grandeur, the greatness of tragedy, all or nothing, that is the price. She gathers her strength, focuses, concentrates. One last effort. The wind is singing soon it will be over, just one last effort through the pain. She knows her duty. Use the pain for the effort; that's it, use the pain.

Evelyn holds the tiger's head tenderly, then, quickly and cleanly, with all the strength she still owns, all the will of her beating brain, she brings the old convict knife up to the throat, and coldly, savagely, cuts it through to the bone.

Following his instinct as much as the map route fixed in his mind, Joseph emerges from the pencil pine forest, now almost at the end of the toughest most sustained trek he has ever attempted. Adrenalin has largely powered him and even at this stage is still coursing through his system, more so, as he slogs up the final stretch to Dixon-Kingdom hut. He almost lost it coming down to the creek before the climb to the Walls, almost turned back. Never would he have attempted something like this in such weather without an overriding imperative, and that imperative, vague but very real, now looms before him in various possible guises. Wind and snow smack into him, roaring down the valley. He bends into it doggedly. She has to be in the hut. He will claim he decided to visit her and got caught and had to keep on. It sounds a bit lame, but it doesn't matter if she is all right and his intimations are wrong.

There is a high drift of snow against the door but fortunately, it opens inwards. Still he can't move it; there is some blockage. He yells out her name against the storm and applies his shoulder and all his weight and it budges. When the crack is wide enough, he squeezes in. She is lying curled on the floor in front of the dead fireplace. He races over, checks her breath, speaks her name, and she moves slightly at his presence. She is bent over something, a kind of curved knife. He tries to take it from her but she resists fiercely and then he sees that her right leg is badly cut. He throws her sleeping bag over her and searches for a first aid kit. There is one on the ledge above the bed. She hardly responds as he cuts away the jeans, cleans the wound as best he can and dresses it. The cut is deep but has not reached the femoral artery and although there is a fair bit of blood, it is probably not as bad as it looks.

The radio is working, useless in the storm, but in time the storm will pass and he'll get help in. There is wood and food. He wedges the door back shut with the stone, starts a small fire, and gets in with her under the bag. She is cold, but her pulse is normal; it doesn't feel like hypothermia, he doesn't know what is wrong. He holds her close and she shifts a little to accommodate him and moans softly. He can't tell what has happened here, but he will see her through this. Of that much, at least, he is certain.